FIC
PAR

Park, Barbara.

Don't make me smile.

$10.52

DATE DUE	BORROWER'S NAME	ROOM NO.
JAN 14 '88	Laura	6
FEB 2 '88	Donald	2
MAR 18 '88	Valerie	6
APR 13 '88	Simona	6

FIC
PAR

Park, Barbara.

Don't make me smile.

CHARLIE HICKLE decides he'd rather live in a tree when his parents tell him they're getting a divorce. DIVORCE. Charlie runs to his dictionary to find out what it really means: *a complete separation.* How could they ruin his life this way? Don't they know he'll go nuts?

Charlie's confusion turns to rebellion as he makes some plans of his own. He refuses to eat his mother's nightly macaroni dinners, thinks up rude comments about the smelly furniture in his father's rundown apartment, sets up big-mouth MaryAnn Brady to break the news at school, and pulls a gagging act when his father takes him to the zoo.

Then Charlie finds a friend in a most unexpected person. Slowly but surely, he decides he's not going nuts after all. But not before he makes one last attempt to get his parents back together again. Fortified with a strong will and a sense of humor, Charlie just won't give up!

Divorce is not a laughing matter, but readers can't help laughing at Charlie's wise-cracking attitude as his world is falling apart, macaroni by macaroni. . . .

Don't Make Me Smile

by Barbara Park

ALFRED A. KNOPF · NEW YORK

to my very special friend

This is a Borzoi Book published by Alfred A. Knopf, Inc.

Copyright © 1981 by Barbara Park
Cover illustration copyright © 1981 by Mark Skolsky
All rights reserved under International and Pan-American
Copyright Conventions. Published in the United States by
Alfred A. Knopf, Inc., New York, and simultaneously in Canada
by Random House of Canada Limited, Toronto. Distributed by
Random House, Inc., New York. Manufactured in the United
States of America   4   5   6   7   8   9   10

Library of Congress Cataloging in Publication Data

Park, Barbara. Don't make me smile.

Summary: A young boy has trouble adjusting to his
parents' divorce.
    [1. Divorce—Fiction]   I. Title.
PZ7.P2197Do   1981   [Fic]   81–4880
ISBN 0–394–84978–7   AACR2
ISBN 0–394–94978–1 (lib. bdg.)

Don't Make Me Smile

1

THERE ARE certain things that happen to you that you never forget. I'm not sure why that is. But I know it's true. For example, no matter how old I get, I'll never forget the first time I was in a school program.

I was in the first grade chorus. And since I was a very short first grader, I got to stand in the front row where everyone could see me.

Boy, I really thought I was hot stuff. I stood up there and sang my guts out. I even used my hands the way the singers on television do.

When it was all over, the audience started clapping like crazy. It really made me feel great. I must have bowed about two hundred times. Even while we were walking back to the room, I was still bowing.

I love going back to the room after a school program. You always get to horse around with the other kids until your parents come pick you up. The teacher tells you to calm down, but at night she doesn't really care. She only gets paid to keep you calm during the day.

Pretty soon, I saw my mother hurrying in the door. She was walking so fast, my father couldn't keep up with her. I could tell she was pretty excited about my performance.

Wow! I thought to myself. I must have been even better than I thought! My mother looks like she wants my autograph or something!

As soon as she spotted me, my mother ran over and bent down beside me. I closed my eyes and got ready for one of her big fat kisses. But instead, she leaned over and whispered, "Charles, your zipper was down."

I looked down. And there, sticking out of my navy blue pants, was this big fat wad of underwear all bunched up in my zipper.

All I could think of was how stupid I must have looked on stage in front of all those people. How can you look like a big singing star with a bunch of underwear hanging out of your pants?

So I started to cry.

Okay, I know that there are a lot of first graders who wouldn't have cared one bit. They would have just zipped up and forgotten all about it. But that's not the kind of kid I am. To me, underwear is real private stuff. I don't even like my cat to see me in it.

After I finished crying, I yelled at my mother. Anytime you're upset, you're supposed to yell at your mother. They expect it. It's part of their job.

4

"It's all your fault!" I said, sobbing, as I reached down and pulled up my zipper. "You're the one who made me so short!"

My mother tried to quiet me down. A couple of the other parents who had come in began to stare. My father started looking around the room, pretending he didn't know me.

"Sh!" said my mother. "You don't have to shout. Now . . . what in the world does being short have to do with your fly being down?" she asked quietly.

"If you didn't make me so short, I would never have had to stand in the front row. And if I wasn't in the front row, no one could have seen that my zipper was down," I sputtered.

I guess I shouldn't have yelled so loud. Benjamin Fowler's parents started to laugh. My father left the room and headed for the car.

"Charles, please!" said my mother, hurrying me out the door. "I'm sorry you're so upset about this. But I don't think it's fair to blame me just because you forgot to zip your fly."

"And don't call it my fly!" I shouted.

Fly. Isn't that just about the stupidest name you've ever heard for a zipper?

My parents finally took me home and put me to bed. My father came in and gave me a little talk on zippers. He told me that being caught with your zipper down is just part of wearing pants. He also told me I would get used to it.

Well, he was wrong. I'm almost eleven years old

now, and I'm still not used to it.

My mother says it's because I'm too sensitive.

Sensitive means that certain things bother you a lot more than they bother most people. For instance, whenever our family watches a real sad movie on TV, I'm always the first one to start blubbering. I try not to. But just when I think I've got myself under control, someone in the movie goes and dies. That's when the blubbering starts.

Sensitive also means that you get your feelings hurt easily. I know this is true. It happens to me all the time. In fact, it just happened again a few weeks ago.

It was my father's birthday. And if there's one thing around our house I love, it's birthdays.

But this one was going to be even more special than any other. For the first time, I was allowed to buy him a present completely on my own. I didn't even have to check with my mother first.

A few days before my dad's birthday, Mom drove me to the shopping center to buy his gift. She waited in the parking lot while I ran in to get it. It didn't take long at all. I knew exactly what I wanted.

As soon as I got it home, I ran to my room to wrap it. I was afraid if I didn't wrap it right away my mother would look in the box while I was in school. I don't mean to make my mother seem like a sneak or anything. It's just that sometimes it's better not to test her.

I really can't explain why I wanted to keep this

6

whole thing such a secret. I guess it just made it more special that way.

Anyway, when my father's birthday finally came, I just couldn't wait for him to open my gift. As he started to unwrap it, my heart began to beat very fast. I felt kind of dumb getting so excited about it. But I just couldn't help it.

Slowly Dad lifted the lid of the box and peeked under the tissue paper.

I knew right away that I was in trouble. I could tell by the look on his face.

"Oh, boy! Look at this, would you?" he said, smiling. "Gee whiz, Charlie, this is just great!"

But he didn't fool me a bit. Because I happen to know that whenever someone opens a present and say, "Oh, boy, look at this," it only means one thing. They don't know what it is.

Think about it. What do you say when you open up a new shirt? Simple. You say, "Oh boy! A new shirt!" And when you open up a new game, you say, "Oh boy! A new game!" But, if you're not exactly sure what it is you're looking at, *that's* when you say, "Oh boy! Look at this!"

My father took his present out of the box and began looking at it more carefully. I could tell he was trying very hard to figure out what it was. He unfolded it and put his hand inside. All he kept saying was "Wow, Charlie, I've always wanted one of these things!"

If you ask me, he was making a fool of himself.

Finally, I couldn't stand it anymore. "It doesn't go on your hand, Dad," I said, sounding a little disgusted. "It goes on your head. It's a chef's hat. You're supposed to wear it outside when you barbeque."

"A chef's hat!" said my father, laughing loudly. "Of course! A chef's hat!"

Then, he put it on his head.

"Just call me Chef Boy·ar·dee!" he said, trying to talk in a dumb Italian accent.

He and my mother were both laughing. I wasn't. And the reason I wasn't laughing was simple. It was not supposed to be a funny gift.

If I had wanted to get him a funny gift, I would have bought him a rubber hot dog.

Anyway, by this time my feelings were really hurt and I felt like I was going to cry. I guess my father saw I was getting upset. I'm not always very good at hiding my feelings.

He took off the hat and stopped making jokes. Then he came over and hugged me.

"Thanks a lot, Charlie," he said. "I really do like it. As a matter of fact, I think I'll cook a steak tonight so I can wear it right away."

"Sure, Dad," I answered, trying to act cool. But inside, I felt awful.

Anyway, since his birthday, my father has worn his chef's hat twice. But, if you want to know the truth, I think he only puts it on when he knows I'm around.

And, if that's true, then I guess I won't be seeing him wear it very much. Because, two weeks after his birthday, my father moved out of the house.

He and my mother are getting a divorce.

DIVORCE—A DEFINITION

Divorce. To me, that word never really meant much. I think it's one of those words like *death.* You know that a lot of people do it, but as long as it's not you, you don't pay much attention.

As a matter of fact, I don't ever remember seeing *divorce* spelled before. I'm positive it's never been on any of my spelling lists at school. Come to think of it, neither has death. I guess you're supposed to learn how to spell all the sad words on your own.

So I looked it up in my dictionary. It said: divorce/də-ˈvōrs/n. 1. a complete legal breaking up of a marriage. 2. complete separation.

Well, that may be what the dictionary thinks divorce is, but I'll tell you what it really is. . . .

Divorce is like watching your mother back the car over your brand new bicycle. You know what's about to happen, but there's nothing you can do about it. So you just stand there and watch the tires of the car crush your bike as flat as a pancake. And you get this terrible, sick feeling inside you, like you're going to throw up.

You don't know what to do, so you start to cry.

Your mother says she's sorry, but it doesn't help.
Nothing helps.

It's all smashed to pieces, and it will never be the same.

It's too late. . . .

That's divorce.

2

SO FAR, one of the worst things about my parents'
divorce is that I'm supposed to go around smiling all
the time. When they were together, I never had to
smile unless I felt like it. But now, ever since they
split up, I have to keep looking real jolly all the
time. If I don't, it makes them feel guilty.

"Cheer up. Cheer up." That's all my mother
keeps saying. Then, she tries to make me smile. If
there's one thing I really hate, it's having someone
try to make you smile when you don't want to.

"Come on," she says, "let me see a little smile."

I try not to. But I know she won't leave me alone
until I do it. So finally, I just shoot her a stupid grin
to get her off my back.

But . . . my mother isn't the only one who keeps
trying to make me smile. My father is just as bad.
He even did it the night he told me about the
divorce.

He knocked on my door and asked if he could
come in. I really could kick myself for not asking

11

him what he wanted. He would have said, "I want to talk to you about the divorce your mother and I are getting."

Then I could have said, "Well, in that case, you can't come in."

And he would have said, "Okay, then, if that's the way you feel about it, I guess we won't get one after all."

And we would have all lived happily ever after. Instead, I just unlocked my door and let him in.

When Dad came into the room, he walked over and sat down on my bed beside me. He had this real serious look on his face, like something terrible had just happened. It really got me scared.

"There's something very important that I have to tell you, Charlie," he said.

By this time, I was sure that someone had died.

"Was it Grandma?" I asked nervously.

My father looked puzzled. "Was what Grandma?" he asked.

"The one who died . . . was it Grandma?" I repeated.

"Oh no, Charles," he said. "It's nothing like that. No one has died."

"Boy," I said, smiling, "that's a relief! For a minute there, you really had me scared!"

"Sorry, Charlie," he said.

Whenever anyone says, "Sorry, Charlie," it always makes me feel like that tuna fish on the TV commercials. Dad and I usually laugh about it. But this time he didn't even smile.

"Charles," he began, "what I'm about to tell you is very, very hard for me."

As soon as he said this, I started getting scared all over again.

"And I know that I'm not going to be able to explain this as well as I want to," he said, "but I'll do the best I can."

He didn't even wait for me to ask, "Explain what?"

"For a long time now," he continued, "your mother and I haven't been very happy living here together."

"What do you mean?" I interrupted, surprised. "You always act okay to me."

"I mean that when your mother and I got married," he said, "we loved each other very much. And, we thought that we would always feel that way. But sometimes things don't always work out the way we want them to. And even though two people care about each other, they're not always happy living together.

"They try, Charlie, but it just doesn't always work. And after a while they decide to make some changes so that they can both be happy again."

My father stopped talking for a moment and looked at me.

"Do you understand what I'm saying, son?" he asked.

"Sort of," I answered. "You think that you and

Mom need to do something to make yourselves happier."

"That's right, Charlie, we do," he said.

Now, here is where I made my next big mistake. I asked an extremely stupid question.

"Well," I asked, "what are you going to do?"

God, I wish I had never asked that! If I hadn't asked it, maybe he would never have said what he said. Maybe he would have changed his mind.

My father took a big deep breath and waited a minute. Then he spoke.

"We've decided to get a divorce," he said quietly.

I just sat there staring at him. I couldn't even speak. He reached out and put his arms around me. He must have thought that I was going to start blubbering.

But I fooled him. I didn't. I don't know why I didn't. I just didn't.

All I could do was just stare at him.

Have you ever noticed that when you stare at somebody long enough, it makes them nervous? And when people get nervous, they say very stupid things. I know this is true. Because after I stared at my father for a while, he said the stupidest thing in the whole world.

"Are you okay?" he asked.

Now, just think about what a stupid question that is. Your own father comes into your room, sits down on your bed, and calmly tells you that he and your mother are going to destroy your entire life. Then,

14

he smiles and asks you if you're okay.

STUPID! STUPID! STUPID!

As a matter of fact, it was such a stupid question, it deserved a stupid answer.

"Sure, Dad, I'm just fine," I answered.

"Of course you are," he said. Then he took his hand and rumpled my hair. I hate that. My hair is usually messy enough without having someone rumple it even more.

"Well," said my father, "I think I've told you just about enough for one night. I know this is hard on you. It's hard on all of us. But I don't want you to worry, Charlie. It's all going to work out okay. I just know it is."

He reached over and hugged me again.

"Could you give me just a little smile to show me you're okay?"

This time I didn't try to fight it. I just shot him my usual dumb grin and got it over with.

My father got up and walked to the door.

"We'll talk about this again tomorrow after you've had a chance to think about it," he said, closing the door behind him.

"Good night, son," he said.

"Good night," I yelled.

I waited a couple of minutes to make sure he was gone.

Then I ran into the bathroom and threw up.

3

I'M NOT SURE how long I stayed in the bathroom that night. But it was long enough to make my mother nervous.

"Charles, are you okay?" she called, knocking on the door.

I don't know why she and my father aren't happy. They sure are a lot alike. They both ask the same stupid questions.

"Great," I shouted. "I'm just great."

I looked in the mirror. I wasn't great. My face was as white as a sheet. All I needed was a couple of fangs and I would have looked just like Count Dracula.

I started the water in the tub. "I'm taking a bath," I yelled.

"Well, if you need anything, just holler," she said.

I do need something, Mom, I thought to myself. I need two parents who care about me. I need you and Dad to stay together. That's what I need. But I didn't say it.

I must have stayed in the tub for an hour. I even washed my hair. I figured that if I could get it looking clean and fluffy, maybe I wouldn't look so much like Dracula. But by the time I got out, my skin was so wrinkled I looked even worse.

I put on my pajamas and slowly opened the bathroom door. I wanted to make sure my mother wasn't hanging around the hall waiting for me to come out.

I just wanted to be left alone.

The coast was clear. Quickly, I dashed into my bedroom and locked the door behind me.

I'm going to bed now," I hollered to my mother through the door. But, as it turned out, I didn't need to shout at all. When I turned around, she was sitting on my bed waiting for me.

I could tell she had been crying. Her nose was all red and her eyes were real puffy-looking. She looked awful.

I wanted to tell her to get out of my room, but I was afraid she would start crying again. And if my father ever saw her looking that awful, he'd leave for sure.

"Do you want to talk about it?" she asked.

I didn't answer.

"Charles," she said, "I know this is a big shock for you, and it's very hard for you to understand. But it's hard for me, too."

Then, a couple of tears rolled down her cheek.

All I can say is that if she was trying to make me

17

feel better, she was doing one lousy job.

I wanted her to leave. It was all that I could think about.

I didn't say anything to her. I just unlocked my door and pointed to the hall. This meant for her to go.

But she didn't. She just sat there.

So I left instead.

I heard my father in the bedroom. I went to his door and looked in. I could tell he was surprised to see me. He was standing there holding two suitcases.

Suddenly, I felt very angry. How could they do this to me? How could two people who were supposed to love me just ruin my life like this?

My father gave me a little smile. "I guess I'll be staying in a motel for a couple of days," he said. "I'll come get you tomorrow and we'll talk. Okay?"

I didn't answer. I was too mad. Instead, I just stood there staring at him holding those suitcases.

Finally, he put them down and walked over to me. "Everything will be okay, Charlie," he said. "I promise you it will."

I just stared.

I could tell that I was beginning to make him feel uncomfortable again.

I was glad.

He picked up his suitcases. "I'll see you tomorrow," he said.

I followed him as he walked down the hall to the

18

front door. I just kept staring. I wanted to make him feel just as bad as I did. I wanted to make him throw up, too.

As soon as he opened the front door, I started to cry.

"Please don't cry, son," he said.

Since he didn't want me to cry, I tried to cry even harder. Making him feel terrible was the only thing that could make me feel better.

As he walked down the front steps to the car, I followed. Only by now, I had started to blubber.

There's a big difference between just plain crying and blubbering.

Crying is when you make little whimpering noises and tears come out of your eyes. Blubbering is when you make this loud heaving noise, and your nose runs, and everyone in the neighborhood can hear you.

My father kept trying to put his suitcases down and hug me. But I kept backing away. I didn't want him to touch me. All I wanted was to show him how terrible he had made me feel.

Finally, he just got in his car and drove away.

I went back inside and ran to my room. My mother was still on my bed. And to make matters worse, she was still crying.

She was really getting on my nerves. What in the world did she have to cry about? Her parents weren't splitting up!

"I want to be left alone," I said when I saw her.

She didn't argue. She just got up and left.

When the door was closed, I flopped on my bed. I was still crying too, but not blubbering.

All I could think about was how both of them kept asking me if I was okay.

I got up and opened my door.

"AND I'M NOT OKAY!" I screamed. "I'LL NEVER BE OKAY AGAIN!!!!!"

4

WHEN SOMETHING bad happens, people don't all act the same way. Some people go nuts and others just act like nothing has happened at all.

I always used to wonder which kind of person I was. Now I know.

I'm the kind who goes nuts.

I started going nuts that day after my father told me about the divorce.

My mother knocked on my door at the regular time to get me up for school.

"Are you awake, Charles?" she yelled.

I didn't answer. I must admit, I was getting pretty good at not answering. It's really very easy. All you have to do is not open your mouth.

To me, the greatest thing about not answering is that no one can make you do it if you don't want to. That makes it very special. Because when you think about it, there're not too many things your parents can't make you do if they really try hard enough.

Take mowing the lawn for instance. . . .

One time I refused to mow the lawn. It was about a hundred and fifty degrees outside, and the grass was about a foot high.

When my mother told me to go out and cut it, I told her I wanted to wait until it got cooler.

"No, Charles," she ordered, "NOW!"

"NO . . . NOT NOW!" I yelled back.

I don't usually yell at my mother like that. It's not that I'm afraid of her or anything. It's just that she can make things pretty miserable for me if I don't do what she says.

Anyway, it only took about two seconds before my mother came into my room, yanked me by the arm, and pulled me outside.

Then she started the lawn mower, put my hands on the handle, and put her hands on top of them.

Before I knew it, she was walking me all over the yard, making me push the mower.

God, did I ever feel like an idiot! Every once in a while, one of my friends would ride by on his bike and laugh. It was really humiliating.

Anyway, that's the kind of thing parents can make you do. But, there's no way they can make you answer if you don't want to. No way in the world.

Of course, I don't want you to get the idea that I wasn't going to speak at all. Oh no! I was planning to speak all right. But only when I felt like it. And only when I had something really mean to say.

"Come on, Charlie, get up!" she said again. "I

don't want you to miss your bus!"

Can you believe that? She actually thought that I was going to go to school and pretend that nothing had happened!

Boy, was she in for a surprise!

I heard her go into the kitchen to start breakfast. But in a couple of minutes, she was right back at my door. Sometimes my mother reminds me of a boomerang.

"Charlie, your breakfast is ready," she yelled for the third time. "Let's go!"

I still didn't answer.

"Charlie?" she called. "CHARLIE? ANSWER ME!"

My mother was getting frantic. And I think I know why. She was probably thinking that I was so upset about the divorce that I killed myself or something. I know that sounds stupid. But I've actually heard of kids doing that sort of thing.

But not me. No way. I may have gone a little bit nuts, but I sure wasn't crazy! Dying is a lot worse than divorce. Just thinking about it made me feel all spooky inside. It also gave me an idea.

My mother got the key to my door and opened it as fast as she could. When she came into my room, I was lying there very, very still.

She ran over and pulled the sheet off me.

"CHARLIE?" she shouted, shaking me. "ARE YOU OKAY? WAKE UP! WAKE UP!"

I didn't move a muscle.

My mother screamed, "OH MY GOD!" and ran out of the room.

As soon as she was gone, I sat up.

A second later, she was back. Just like a boomerang.

"Oh, thank God, Charles!" she screamed, again. "I thought you were . . . I mean, I thought something terrible had happened to you!"

She sat down on my bed and hugged me as tightly as she could. But my mother's not dumb. And it didn't take her long to realize that I had just played a very mean trick on her. That's when she got mad.

Parents do this sort of thing all the time. First they're real happy to see that you're all right. But after a couple of minutes, they think they have to punish you.

"How could you do a thing like that to me?" she screeched. "How could you deliberately let me think a terrible thing like that?"

Naturally I didn't answer.

"And, look at you!" she continued. "You're not even dressed yet! Do you know how late it is?!"

Personally, I think that my mother is very strange. She yells just as much for not being dressed as she does for pretending to be dead. To me, pretending to be dead is a lot worse than not being dressed. . . .

"I'm going to say this one more time, Charles,"

24

she shouted. "Get ready for school this minute. And I mean N–O–W!"

You'd think that when your kid is still wearing his pajamas five minutes before the school bus comes, you would understand that he wasn't going to school that day. But not my mother . . . she still wasn't getting the picture.

"I'm not going to school today," I said softly.

"WHAT DO YOU MEAN, YOU'RE NOT GOING TO SCHOOL TODAY?" she said—loudly.

I explained. "That means I'm not getting on the bus. I'm not getting off the bus. I'm not going to my classroom. I'm not sitting down in my seat. I'm not going out for recess. I'm not going to the lunchroom . . ."

"That's enough, Charles," said my mother. "That's just about enough!"

Then, she got up and walked around the room a few minutes. Finally she stopped and sat down on my bed again.

"Look, honey," she began nicely, "I know that you had an awful shock last night. And, I know that you must be very upset about it. But that doesn't give you the right to go around acting horrible to everyone.

"Now, today, after school, your dad is going to pick you up and try to explain things to you better There are a lot of things that he can tell you to help you understand what's happening.

25

"And sooner or later, we're all going to get over this. But it won't make things any easier if we all go around acting terrible to each other. Do you understand what I'm saying?"

Slowly I nodded.

"Good," she said, giving me another hug. "I knew I could count on you. Now, hurry up and get dressed."

"Mom?" I said, as she started for the door. "Could I just finish what I started to say before?"

"Sure, Charlie," she said, "what is it?"

"Well, I just wanted to say that after I don't go to the lunchroom, I'm not going to music. Then I'm not going back to my classroom. I'm not going to get dismissed. And I'm not going to wait for Dad to come get me."

My mother looked very confused.

"But you just told me you were going," she said.

"No, I didn't," I answered.

"Okay, then, Mr. Smart Aleck," she said, getting angry all over again. "Let me put it *this* way. You *are* getting dressed, and you are getting dressed *now*! Do you hear me?"

I didn't answer. Instead, I crawled back under my sheet.

My mother stormed over to my bed and started to shake me.

"You listen to me, young man," she shouted. "I expect you to mind me. I AM STILL YOUR MOTHER!"

26

"No you're not!" I yelled back. "A mother is a person who loves her kids and cares about their feelings. I don't know what you are, but if you ask me, you're sure no mother!"

This time, my mother didn't shout back. Instead, she ran to her bedroom and slammed the door. I think she had started to cry again.

I don't care.

I don't like people who ruin my life.

5

THE REASON that I didn't want to go to school was simple. I didn't want to have to tell my friends that my parents were getting a divorce. I just didn't want to do it.

But refusing to go to school is a lot like mowing the lawn. If your parents really want you to go, they can usually figure out a way to make you. So, while I was lying there in bed, I tried to think of what I would say to my friends if my parents made me go.

One thing was for sure. I didn't want to have to go around saying it a million times. I wanted to say it once and get it over with.

I wondered if our principal, Mr. Kabinski, would let me use the loudspeaker. That would be perfect. I got out of bed and wrote down exactly what I would say:

May I have your attention, please? This is Charles Hickle speaking.

I would like to inform everyone that last night, at

approximately 8:15 P.M., my father came into my room and told me that he and my mother are planning to get a divorce.

Now I know that some of you have already been through this sort of thing, and it didn't really bother you. But I also know that different people react to bad news in different ways. As for me . . . I have gone nuts.

I hope this will explain why some of you saw my mother dragging me to school today. And I also hope it will explain why I am wearing my pajamas.

I read my announcement over and over again. It sounded pretty good. But I really didn't think I would ever get to use it.

First of all, I didn't think that my mother was feeling strong enough to drag me to school. Crying takes a lot out of you.

And second of all, I was sure that Mr. Kabinski would never let some nut in his pajamas use the loudspeaker. That's why I decided to think of some other way to handle it.

Unfortunately, my next idea wasn't much better than the first one. I decided to simply tell everyone that my father was away on a business trip.

But sooner or later, I knew that someone would say, "Wow! Your dad sure has been gone a long time. How long does his business trip last, anyway?"

Then I would have to say, "He's on one of those business trips that last your whole life."

And even though my friends seem pretty dopey sometimes, they're still smart enough to know that no one stays on a business trip for his whole life.

There was only one thing left to do. I got out of bed and went into the kitchen to call MaryAnn Brady.

MaryAnn Brady lives next door. I don't like her very much, but sometimes she comes in handy. MaryAnn is one of those people you can always count on when you have a secret. If you tell your secret to MaryAnn, she will have it spread all over the school by lunchtime. It never fails. Good old MaryAnn. It's nice to have someone you can really count on.

After two rings, MaryAnn answered the phone. I knew she would still be home, because she never takes the bus. Her father drives her to school. I think she likes to stay home extra long in the mornings, just in case anyone wants to call and tell her a last minute secret.

"Hello," she said.

"Hi, MaryAnn. It's Charles," I said.

MaryAnn is also one of those people who doesn't say "hi" after you tell her your name. All she does is breathe.

"Listen, MaryAnn," I continued. "I don't think I'm going to be going to school today."

"So?" she said.

"So, I just wanted to tell you why I'm not going.

It's a big secret, and I don't want anyone else to know."

I could almost see MaryAnn's eyes light up. She really loves secrets.

"What is it, Charlie?" she asked real nicely. "Tell me."

"Okay," I answered, "but first you have to promise not to tell anyone. Not even your mother and father."

"I promise," she said excitedly. "Now what is it?"

"Well, the reason that I won't be going to school today is that last night my parents told me they were getting a divorce."

MaryAnn got so excited, it sounded like she almost dropped the phone.

"ARE YOU KIDDING?" she squealed. "YOUR PARENTS ARE GETTING A DIVORCE? WOW! A DIVORCE!"

Already I was sure that her parents had heard the news. God, what a big mouth!

"Remember, MaryAnn," I said, "you promised not to tell anyone."

But MaryAnn didn't hear me. She had already said good-bye. I guess she really had to hurry, if she was going to tell the whole school by lunchtime.

As soon as I hung up the phone, I started back to my room. Unfortunately, I didn't quite make it. Just as I passed the front door, my father walked in. I guess my mother must have called him.

31

"What's this I hear about you refusing to go to school?" he said quietly.

I looked at him but I didn't say a thing.

"Go get your clothes on," he ordered.

I don't know why, but when my father says to do something, it always sounds like he means it more than my mother does. And the funny part is, he doesn't even have to shout.

So when he said "Go get your clothes on," that's exactly what I did. And to tell you the truth, I was kind of glad I did. At least now, if my mother dragged me to school, I wouldn't have to sit around in my pajamas.

After I was dressed, my father came into my room and sat down on my bed.

"Why are you acting like this, Charlie?" he asked, reaching out to pat me on the leg. "This isn't like you. You're usually so reasonable and easy to talk to."

I shrugged my shoulders.

"What are you thinking? I can't help you if I don't know what you're thinking," he continued.

I just looked at him.

"Do you think that your mother and I don't care about you? Is that what you think? Do you think that we don't love you anymore?" he asked.

I shrugged my shoulders again.

"Well, if that's what you're thinking, you're wrong," he said. "You're very, very wrong. Your mother and I love you very much."

32

Suddenly, I couldn't be quiet any longer.

"Do you call ruining my life loving me?" I asked angrily. "Is that what you call it?"

"We're not going to ruin your life, Charlie," he said. "We're just changing things a little bit."

Boy, did that ever make me mad!

"Changing things a little bit?" I shouted. "Changing things a little bit? Do you call wrecking our whole family changing things a little bit?"

I started to cry. But I kept right on yelling.

"Do you call not having a father around anymore a little change?

"Or maybe you think that just because I'm a kid I'm too stupid to know what divorce means. Maybe you think I'm just too dumb to know that my whole life is ruined!"

"I've never thought that you were stupid, Charlie," said my father quietly.

"Well, then, why do you go around asking me stupid questions, like am I okay? Because for your information, I'm *not* okay. AND I'LL NEVER BE OKAY AGAIN!"

Then I turned over and cried into my pillow.

My father didn't do anything for a while. He just sat there listening to me cry and rubbing my back.

Finally he told me I didn't have to go to school. He also asked if there was anything that he could do for me.

"Yeah," I said, sobbing, "you could stay with Mom and me."

THE NEXT DAY I decided to go back to school. Staying home just never turns out to be as much fun as I think it will. Usually I get so bored, I end up wishing I had gone to school in the first place.

When I got to class, I was very proud of MaryAnn Brady. Just as I predicted, everyone already knew about the divorce. The first person who mentioned it was my teacher, Mrs. Fensel. She walked over to my desk and patted me on the back.

"MaryAnn told me about your problem at home, Charles," she said. "If there's anything I can do to help you, please let me know."

It made me feel kind of embarrassed.

"Sure . . . okay . . . thanks a lot," I mumbled.

At lunchtime I found the table where MaryAnn was sitting.

"Congratulations, MaryAnn," I said. "You really did a great job."

"Congratulations for what?" she asked.

"For being such a big fat blabbermouth," I

answered. "Thanks to you, the whole school knows about the divorce."

MaryAnn looked at me for a second. Then she said something that every single blabbermouth in the whole world always says right after they finish blabbing a big secret.

"I didn't tell anyone!" she shouted. "HONEST!"

"Why can't you just learn to keep your big yap shut, MaryAnn?" I asked angrily.

I wanted to make sure she thought I was really mad about it. Blabbermouths only like to tell secrets if they're not supposed to. If MaryAnn ever found out that I wanted her to blab, she'd stop doing it. And like I said before, sometimes she can come in very handy.

"I didn't tell anyone," she insisted.

"Then how come about a thousand people came up to me this morning and told me that they knew all about the divorce?" I asked. "And how come they all said it was you who told them? How do you explain that, Blabbo?" I asked.

"Anyone who told you that," said MaryAnn, "is a big fat liar!"

"Gee, MaryAnn," I answered, "I'm sure that Mrs. Fensel will be glad to know that you think she's a big fat liar. Because when I got to school today, Mrs. Fensel told me she knew all about my 'problem.' And, she also told me that she got the news from you."

Then I got up from the table. "Excuse me for a

minute, Blabbo," I said. "I think I'll go tell Mrs. Fensel that she's a big fat liar."

MaryAnn's face turned as white as a sheet.

I walked over to the table where Mrs. Fensel was eating lunch. MaryAnn watched me as I tapped Mrs. Fensel on the shoulder. I whispered something in her ear and pointed over to where Mary-Ann was sitting.

God! You should have seen MaryAnn squirm! After a couple of minutes, she packed up her things and ran out of the lunchroom. I didn't see her for a while after that. But someone told me that she had run into the bathroom and cried.

I don't know what she was crying about. All I did was show Mrs. Fensel where I was sitting and ask her if I could have a few extra minutes to eat my lunch. I told her I was having a hard time swallowing. I was, too. Being upset always makes it hard to swallow.

I didn't have to worry about swallowing too much when I was at home. After my father left, the meals that my mother made were so terrible that you didn't want to swallow them.

I should have reported her to the health department. I think there's a law to make mothers feed their children good dinners. If there's not a law, there ought to be.

The first week that my father was gone was the worst. I remember when she called me to supper the first night. I was really hungry. I had spent the whole day in my room thinking about how ruined my life was.

For lunch I had only been able to eat half an apple. I wanted more but I was having a hard time swallowing.

When I got to the dinner table, I thought that maybe I had made a mistake. Maybe it wasn't dinnertime after all. The only thing on my plate was a hard-boiled egg and two slices of bread.

"Didn't you just call me to dinner?" I asked.

"Yes," answered my mother. "Sit down and make yourself an egg sandwich."

The thought of eating a dried-up egg sandwich made me sick. I'd rather eat a frog.

"Don't we have any soup?" I asked.

"Listen, Charles," said my mother, "don't give me a hard time, okay? Please, just eat your sandwich and drink a glass of milk. I'll make you a better dinner tomorrow night."

She did too. The next night, she made one of those macaroni and cheese dinners . . . and the next night . . . and the next night. . . . As a matter of fact, my mother cooked macaroni and cheese for dinner four nights in a row.

I used to like macaroni and cheese a lot. Now I can't stand the stuff. It's just one more thing that this divorce has ruined for me.

The whole problem of my mother's meals was really making me mad. It's not that I wanted to eat. In fact, I really didn't feel much like eating at all.

It's just that I thought my mother could have tried a little harder. When she didn't try, it made me feel like she didn't care about me.

The fourth night she served macaroni and cheese, I finally told her how I felt.

"What are we having for dinner tonight?" I asked, as if I didn't know.

"I'm heating up that leftover macaroni and cheese," she said, stirring it around in the pot.

"Don't we have any soup yet?" I asked.

"Listen, Charles," said my mother. "I'll get some next week. I just haven't felt much like going to the grocery store. Besides, I thought you loved macaroni and cheese."

"I used to," I answered. "But, that was before I ate three hundred million macaronis in a row. Can't we just go to the store and get some soup?"

"Stop arguing, Charlie," she said, plopping a big spoonful of macaroni and cheese on my plate.

"No, thank you," I said, pushing it away. "If I put one more little macaroni in my mouth, I'll gag."

I felt myself starting to get very angry.

"I'm not a pig, you know, Mother," I said.

"What in the world are you talking about?" she asked. "I never said you were a pig."

"I mean I'm not a pig, and you can't just throw some slop on the table and expect me to eat it."

My mother got mad. Mothers really hate for their dinners to be called 'slop.'

"Go to your room!" she shouted.

Quickly, I got up and ran to my room. I gathered some of my things together and stuffed them into an old shoe box. I would have stuffed them into my old gym bag, but it got broken at Harold Stengler's spend-the-night party. Harold and another kid were trying to zip me inside it when the sides busted.

As soon as I was packed, I spotted my dumb helicopter beanie. It was hanging on my bulletin board. My father had bought it for me at the state fair a couple of years ago. It's probably the dumbest thing I own, but for some reason it always makes me laugh. Quickly, I grabbed it and stuck it on my head. I figured if I ever needed a good laugh, it was now.

Then, I quietly opened my window and left.

7

RUNNING AWAY from home is something that I'd always wanted to do. I would have tried it a long time ago, but I never really had a good enough reason. Until the divorce came along, my parents had never done anything bad enough to make me leave.

Once in a while I got sent to my room. And a couple of times they took my allowance away. But that's about it. I always thought it would sound stupid if you had to tell your friends that you ran away from home because your parents wouldn't give you the dollar they owed you that week. . . .

But divorce . . . now, *there's* a reason to run away.

When I climbed out my window that night, I've got to admit, I was pretty excited. Being out alone after dark is a pretty neat feeling. It makes you feel real sneaky, like a cat burglar or something.

I started walking down the street very slowly. I didn't run. When you run away from home, the worst possible thing you can do is run. Running always makes you look like you're doing something wrong. If you ask me, I think they ought to call it *walking* away from home. I bet a lot less kids would get caught if they walked.

The most important thing about leaving home is that you've got to have a plan. If you don't have a plan, you might as well just stay home.

As for me, I've always known exactly what I would do if I ever left home. I got the idea from a TV show I saw a couple of years ago.

The show was about these two little kids who ran away from an orphanage. They didn't have anywhere to go, so they decided to live in a tree in the park. It turned out to be the perfect place to live. No one found out about them for months.

When I got to the end of my street, I turned and headed toward the park. We only live about three blocks from there, so it didn't take long before I arrived. And once I was there, finding the tree I wanted to live in was a snap. I chose one right next to the boy's bathroom.

It was a big tree and looked as though it would be pretty easy to climb, so I held the shoe box under my arm and started up.

Climbing the tree turned out to be no problem at all. I've always been an expert tree climber. My legs aren't very long, but I have great balance.

After I got up about ten feet, I stopped to look down. It was perfect! The limbs were so thick and bushy, I knew no one could spot me.

I picked out a nice fat branch to sit on and carefully placed the shoe box next to me. Then I looked inside. There were three pairs of underpants, a toothbrush, a pair of pajamas, and no toothpaste.

"God! What stupid stuff to pack!" I said right out loud.

Oh, well, it didn't really matter anyway. The important thing was that I didn't have to listen to any more of the divorce talk. I thought about my mother and wondered what she was doing. By now, she had probably already called the police and filed a missing-persons report. Who cares? I thought. Not even the best detective in the world could have spotted me in that tree. I wasn't worried. I was completely safe.

I leaned back and tried to make myself comfortable. It was getting late and I had to figure out a way to sleep. On the TV show I had seen, the kids had built a tree house. But naturally I hadn't had time to get to that yet, so I just had to do the best I could.

The first thing you need when you're trying to get comfortable is a pillow, I took my shoe box and placed it between my head and the tree trunk.

"Ahhhhh," I said out loud, "now that's more like it!" But it wasn't any use. I've never been very good at pretending. The shoe box didn't feel at all like a pillow. It felt like a shoe box.

I would have tried using my pajamas for a pillow

but I needed to use them as a blanket. It had really started to get chilly. It was April, but if you ask me, it felt a lot more like January. This gave me one more reason to be angry at my parents. If they really loved me, they would have waited until July to get divorced.

I tried scrunching up into a little ball to keep warm, but it didn't help at all. Finally, I took two pairs of underpants out of the box and wrapped one around each hand. When I get cold, my hands are always the first part of my body to freeze. Next comes my ears. And this time was no exception.

I had no choice. I took off my beanie and put it in my box. Then I pulled out the last pair of underwear and put them on my head. I pulled them way down so they would cover my ears. I never thought I would do anything that dumb. But when you're cold, you don't care if you're dumb.

It wasn't long before I started shivering. One time during science class my teacher told us that shivering is the way your body tries to warm itself. Well, I hate to tell her, but she's wrong. Shivering makes you feel even colder. There's no way that you can hear your teeth chattering and convince yourself that you're getting all toasty warm. No way.

"BRR!" I said, right out loud. "BRR, BRR, BRR!"

When you're freezing, sometimes saying 'brr" makes you feel better. At least, it helps more than shivering.

I promised myself that the next morning, I would

sneak home and bring back a blanket. Meanwhile, I tried not to think about how cold and uncomfortable I was. The main thing was that I was out of the house, and no one could ever find me.

"BRR!" I said again.

"Cold up there?" said a voice.

I panicked! Who said that? Who was down there? I got very quiet and listened.

"YOOOOWHOOOO," said the voice, again. "Charlie Hickle? Are you up there, Charlie?"

This was impossible. No one could have possibly known that I was in that tree! Carefully I peeked down between the branches. It was really dark, but I could see someone's shadow.

"CHARLIE . . ." called the voice again. "CHARLIEEEEEEE. . . ."

IT WAS MY MOTHER! Oh, no! How could this be? No one could see me. I was sure of it!

Wait a minute, I thought. Maybe she's just bluffing! Of course! That was it! She just came to the park and started calling my name, hoping that I would give myself away! She was bluffing!

"Hey up there," she called again. "You with the underwear on your head. . . ."

She wasn't bluffing.

This was, without a doubt, the most embarrassing thing that had ever happened to me. It was even worse than singing with my zipper down.

"Go away!" I shouted. "Leave me alone!"

"Don't be silly, Charlie," said my mother. "You

can't stay up there all night. If you don't come down, I'll have to call the fire department."

God! She was treating me like a cat!

"Go away!" I said again. "I live here! I'm not coming down, Mother. And, stop treating me like a cat!"

"For heaven's sake, Charlie," shouted my mother, "you're being ridiculous! You can't live in a tree! Just think about how silly that is. How will you keep warm?"

"I'll shiver!" I shouted. (It was all I could think of.)

"Oh, wonderful," said my mother, "and what exactly do you plan to eat up there?"

"Nuts and berries," I yelled back.

God! I wish I hadn't said that! Now I sounded like a squirrel. My mother thought so, too.

"Good grief, Charles," she said, "you're acting just like a squirrel. . . . Okay, then," she continued, "you leave me no other choice. I'm going to go call the fire department to get you down."

I saw her start walking away. I didn't really think that she would call the fire department, but there are some things you don't want to take a chance on. Having a big hook and ladder truck come drag you out of a tree is one of them.

"Okay, okay," I shouted, "You win. Don't call the fire department. I'm coming down."

I started down. On the way, I remembered to grab my pajamas from the limb where they had fallen. It's too bad I didn't remember to take the underwear off my head, too.

When my mother saw me, she started to giggle. She was trying not to, but let's face it, I looked ridiculous.

"I'm sorry, honey," she said, pulling it off my head. "I know you must be freezing."

Then, she put her arm around me, and we started walking home. I was pretty proud of myself. I didn't even start crying. I just kept quiet and walked.

I was also proud of my mother. For once in her life, she kept quiet, too.

When we got home, I headed for the front door. But my mother pulled me over toward the car. We both got in.

She drove to the grocery store and handed me two dollars.

"I'll wait here," she said. "You go pick out the kind of soup you want."

I ran into the store and came back with five cans of chicken-noodle soup. It's my favorite.

On the way home, my mother stopped by McDonald's and bought me a cheeseburger and a large order of fries.

By this time, I had started to feel a lot better. But I was still pretty confused. I just couldn't understand how in the world anyone could have spotted me way up there in that tree.

"Mom, how in the world did you know where to look for me?" I asked, finally.

"It was simple," she answered. "I followed you."

"You mean that you were behind me the whole time?" I asked.

"Yup," she said. "I heard your bedroom window open, so I decided to see what you were doing. Just as I looked in your room, you were climbing out, so I followed you."

"Geez, some cat burglar," I mumbled.

After that, I went to bed. I have to admit it sure did feel a lot better than the tree branch. Those poor squirrels don't know what they're missing.

My mother came in to say good-night. She stayed for a few minutes and gave me a little speech on how we're supposed to talk about our problems, not run away from them. She said if there was anything else bothering me, I should tell her about it.

Well, there was a lot else bothering me, all right, but I didn't feel much like talking about any of it. That is, except for one thing.

"Mom," I said, as she was leaving.

"What is it, Charlie?" she answered. "Is there something else you want to tell me?"

"Yes," I said.

"Well, what is it?" she asked.

"I hope we don't have chicken-noodle soup five nights in a row either," I said.

My mother just shook her head and shut the door.

47

8

THE NEXT DAY was Saturday. It was the first Saturday since I had learned about the divorce.

Usually on Saturdays, I get up early and start calling my friends to find something to do. But this time, I didn't really feel like it.

I stayed in bed until my mother called me for breakfast. I wasn't hungry, but I could tell by the smell coming from the kitchen that she had made something special. I think she was still trying to make up for all that macaroni and cheese.

When I got to the table, I saw that she had fixed french toast with cinnamon and sugar. It's one of my favorites.

"Sit down and eat, honey," said my mother, smiling. "Your father will be picking you up in a few minutes."

This was news to me. I hadn't even seen my father since Monday morning.

"What's he picking me up for?" I asked. "I wish someone would ask me first. I might not feel like being picked up."

The more I thought about it, the angrier I got.

"It really makes me mad when people go around picking you up when you don't want to be picked up in the first place!" I said loudly. "If you ask me, it's just plain rude!"

My mother tried to calm me down.

"Charlie, it's time that you and your dad had a chance to talk. He's been waiting all week to speak to you. But he wanted to let you settle down before he came over."

"What makes you think that I'm settled down?" I asked. "If I was settled down, do you think I would have run away to live in a tree? Does that sound like a kid who is settled down? I don't want to see him."

"Well, I guess it doesn't matter whether you want to see him or not, Charles," she said. "He'll be here any minute."

Just about that time, the doorbell rang. I can't tell you how weird it is when your own father starts ringing the doorbell of his own house. It makes him seem more like the mailman than your father. . . .

My mother went to let him in. Then she came into the kitchen, kissed me good-bye, and left the room. I could tell by the way she was acting that she didn't want to be in the same room with my father. I knew exactly how she felt. I didn't either.

My father was the only one who was acting happy. He came bouncing into the kitchen all smiles.

"Good morning, Charlie," he said. "What smells so good in here?"

"French toast," I mumbled.

"French toast?" he asked. "Boy, do I love french toast!"

"Too bad you don't live here anymore," I said. "Then maybe you could have had some."

I held a big bite right out in front of him. It was dripping with maple syrup. Then I stuffed it into my mouth.

I think that my father could plainly see that I wasn't settled down. He stopped being quite as cheery.

"Come on, son," he said, "let's try to get along today, okay? I've got a nice little trip all planned for us."

Oh no! I thought. Not a dumb little trip! I couldn't stand it! It was going to be just like on TV. On TV whenever parents get divorced, the father always gets the kids on the weekends and takes them on stupid little "trips." They always go someplace real corny, like the zoo.

"We're going to the zoo," he said.

God! I knew it! Just like on TV! Well, no thanks . . . not me. . . .

"I hate the zoo," I said. "The smell at the zoo makes me puke."

My father looked disappointed. "Aw, come on, Charles," he said. "We'll have a great time."

"What's so great about seeing a lot of weird,

stinking animals?" I asked, angrily.

My father ignored me. As a matter of fact, he didn't say another word. But after I finished eating, he took me by the arm and led me to the car. I didn't really think that after all the mean stuff I had said that he would still take me to the zoo. But I was wrong. We went to the zoo, anyway.

As soon as we got out of the car, I started to sniff the air and make gagging noises. My father still ignored me. He paid the money at the gate and we went in.

I kept right on gagging and started holding my nose. By this time, a lot of people had stopped to stare at me. You'd have thought that they'd never seen anyone gag before.

My father walked over by the lake where all the peacocks hung out. I followed. He sat down in the grass. I just stood there.

"Sit down, Charlie," he said.

"No thanks," I said, still gagging. "I don't usually like to sit down in peacock do-do."

"What are you talking about?" asked my Dad.

"I'm talking about the big pile of peacock poop you just sat down in," I said.

My father jumped up quickly and looked down.

"There's nothing there!" he said.

I just smiled. "April fool," I said. "It was just a little joke."

My father sat back down. Only this time he pulled me down with him.

"I'm tired of your little jokes. I'm tired of the way you're acting. And, most of all, I'm tired of trying to be nice." he growled. "So I'm telling you . . . if you know what's good for you, you will shape up right now."

He meant it. I can always tell when my father has really had enough. He makes his voice sound like it wants to hurt you.

"Now there are a couple of things I want to talk to you about," he continued. "And the first one is about where you're going to live. Your mother and I aren't quite sure what to do with you."

"Great," I said. "Why don't you just give me to Goodwill?" I suggested. "Isn't that what people do with stuff that they don't want anymore?"

"I didn't mean it that way and you know it. Now, will you please shut up and stop feeling sorry for yourself?" he ordered. "Who says that we don't want you?"

I shrugged my shoulders.

"Charlie, the trouble is that we *both* want you. Believe me, no one is trying to dump you. As a matter of fact, I was just going to ask you if you would like to come and live with me for a while. I'd really like to have you. I could sure use some company."

I have to admit this really surprised me. I didn't know what to say.

"Where do you live?" I asked finally.

"I've got an apartment," he answered.

52

"Where is it?" I asked.

"Come on," he said. "I'll show you."

We left the zoo and drove for about twenty minutes. Finally, he stopped in front of a dumpy old building. I figured we were probably out of gas. At least that's what I was hoping. I couldn't imagine my father living in such a rundown place.

"Why are we stopping here?" I asked.

"This is it," he answered. "We're here. How do you like it?"

"How do I like what?" I asked. "All I see is that dump over there."

My father looked a little annoyed. "That 'dump' is my apartment," he said. "A friend of mine owns the building and he rented me the apartment on the second floor."

"Some friend," I muttered. But I don't think he heard me.

Naturally, I had already decided that I didn't want to live there. As a matter of fact, I wasn't even sure I wanted to visit. If any of my friends saw me, it would be pretty embarrassing.

My father led me to the stairs around back. We climbed to the second floor. When he unlocked the door to the apartment, he had to give me a little shove to get me to go in.

"Well," he said, "how do you like it?"

"It smells in here, Dad," I said.

I think I hurt his feelings, but I couldn't help it. The place stunk.

"It's just a little musty," he said. "It hasn't been used in a long time. But after I get some new furniture and give it a paint job, I think it will be just fine."

All of a sudden, I didn't feel quite as mad at my father as I had been before. For some reason, knowing that he lived in a dump made me feel a lot better. And for the first time, I began to understand that he and my mother must have been very unhappy together. Because I know that my father would have never moved into a dump unless things were pretty bad for him at home.

I sat down on the couch. But I didn't stay there long. I think that's where the funny smell was coming from. So I got up and moved to the chair. The chair wasn't much better than the couch, but I had run out of furniture to sit on, so I stayed there and just tried not to breathe very much.

"If you and Mom were so unhappy, how come I never heard you guys fight?" I asked.

This was something that really bothered me. I think that if my parents had gone around screaming at each other all the time, I wouldn't have minded if they got divorced. But my parents always acted so normal, I never even knew anything was wrong.

"When two people are unhappy, they don't always scream and fight, Charlie," answered my Dad. "Your mother and I aren't screamers. In fact what we did was probably even worse. We just shut each other out. You might say we just stopped communicating.

"It's very hard to explain what happened to us," he continued. "I'm not even sure if we really know. Your mother and I started out loving each other very much. But over the years, our feelings for each other just seemed to change."

"Why, Dad?" I asked, trying hard to understand. "Why did you let your feelings change?"

"We didn't mean to," he answered. "It just happened. And it happened so slowly that neither one of us even knew it. All we knew was that after a while, we didn't really enjoy being around each other like we did before. But it wasn't until a few weeks ago that we ever really talked about it.

"I wish that we had talked about it sooner," he said. "Then maybe we could have stopped what was happening to us. But we didn't. And now it's too late."

"No, it's not, Dad!" I said. "You could still try, if you wanted to. You're always telling me that a person can do anything if he really wants to badly enough."

"But that's just it, son," he said sadly. "Neither of us wants to try. That's what makes it too late for your mother and me."

My father and I sat there for a long time. We didn't say a word. I didn't want to admit it, but I think I knew what he was saying. The same thing had happened to me before.

A few years ago this kid named Andy Roberts

moved in across the street. At first, I was really happy about it. Andy and I became best friends. We did everything together. My mother said that we were more like twins than just friends.

But after about a year, Andy started getting real interested in insects. It seemed like every time I went over there, all he wanted to do was collect bugs and put them in jars. He kept telling me it was a *fascinating* hobby. I'm not kidding. He really used the word *fascinating*.

Now, I have nothing against bugs. But, after you've put a few bugs in jars, it gets pretty boring. All you do is watch them crawl up the sides and then knock them back down again. Big deal. Real *fascinating*.

Anyway, after a while, I stopped going over there. And now Andy and I hardly even see each other anymore. I don't hate him or anything. And I don't think he hates me. I guess it's like my father said. We just changed.

After a few minutes, my father got up and walked over to the smelly chair where I was sitting.

"Well, how about it," he said. "Would you like to live here with your old Pop?" When he said it, he sounded kind of lonely.

I didn't want to hurt his feelings anymore. He already seemed sad enough. But one thing was for sure. There was no way in the world that I was ever going to move into that stink hole with him. No way.

"Well, Dad," I began, "maybe it would be better if I just stayed with Mom. She probably needs me more than you do."

I really hoped that she hadn't told him about me running away. When someone runs away, it doesn't make them seem very helpful.

"That may be true, Charlie," he said, "but she doesn't need you if you're going to keep acting up. She told me about how you ran away last night."

Good old Mom, I thought. She can never keep anything to herself. I bet when she was little, she was just like MaryAnn Brady.

"I'm not going to run away anymore," I said. "I promise. I just did that because I was mad at her."

"Well, it's your choice, Charlie," said my father. "But I'm not going to have you making things worse for your mother. And remember, if you're not happy there, you are always welcome to live here with me."

I took another whiff of the place. No thank you, I thought to myself. Not on your life. . . .

My father looked at his watch.

"How about some lunch?" he asked.

For once, food sounded pretty good. "Okay," I answered.

"I'm getting to be a pretty good cook," said Dad.

Then he reached into the cabinet and pulled out a box. You guessed it. It was macaroni and cheese. . . .

9

WHEN MY FATHER brought me home that afternoon, I said hello to my mother, and went straight to my room. Once I got there, I sat down on my bed and started to blubber.

It was really weird. I didn't even know I was going to do it. The worst part was, I couldn't stop.

My father was still there. He heard me and came in to see what was wrong. I blubbered that I wanted to be left alone.

When he left the room, I heard him tell my mother that maybe it would be good for me to cry awhile. So they did as I asked and left me alone.

This was the first time that I had cried since Monday. In fact, most of the time, I hadn't really even felt like crying. I guess I had been more mad than sad.

But after seeing my father's apartment, I wasn't as angry anymore. And, I had started to feel real sad about what was happening to our family.

Every time I thought about it, I cried even

harder. I know this makes me sound like a big baby. But, I don't really care. Besides, I think that when you're sensitive, you have more tears than other kids.

All I know is that when my mother called me for dinner, I couldn't eat a thing. I just sat there looking down at my food and sniffling. It was too bad, too. She had made spaghetti, one of my favorites.

I tried to make my mother feel good by eating a couple of noodles, but it was no use. I couldn't swallow. I just sat there with these noodles hanging out of my mouth. Finally, my mother told me I could eat later when I was feeling better. I guess I must have been making her sick.

I left the table and went back to my room. I swallowed the noodles and started crying all over again.

That night I must have even cried in my sleep. Because the next morning my pillow felt real soggy.

It was Sunday, and there wasn't much to do. I got up for a while and wandered around the house. But, I kept ending up back in my room thinking about my dad.

By the time Sunday night rolled around, my mother was getting worried about me. The only time I came out of my room was to get more Kleenex. She even made some chicken-noodle soup and brought it to my room. This was really nice of her. It's too bad I couldn't eat it.

I went to bed early. I thought that maybe if I got a

good night's sleep, I would feel better in the morning. But when the morning came, I still felt lousy. My mother must have known it. She didn't even bother to get me up for school.

About nine o'clock my father dropped by to see how I was doing. At least I thought that's why he came by. Actually, he had another reason. And, it turned out to be a very sneaky one.

"Get your clothes on, son," he said, when he saw that I was still in my pajamas.

"I really don't feel much like going to school today, Dad," I said, blowing my nose. Anyone could see that I wasn't faking.

"I know," said my father. "There's another place that I'd like to take you this morning. Come on and get ready. It's a surprise."

I thought about it while I was getting dressed. At first I wasn't sure that I was in the right mood for surprises, but I decided that anything would be better than lying around on a soggy pillow.

By the time I got in the car, I had decided he was taking me out to breakfast. If there's one thing that always cheers me up, it's going out to breakfast.

We drove for several miles. Finally he pulled the car up in front of a small white building.

"Come on," he said, getting out of the car. "There's someone in here I want you to meet."

It sure didn't look much like a restaurant. I was getting very suspicious.

My father and I went inside the building and down a long narrow hall. When we were almost to the end, he stopped in front of one of the offices.

"Surprise," he said sheepishly. "This is the place."

I looked at the sign on the door. It said:

DR. HENRY T. GIRARD
Child Psychologist

"Oh, no! Not a shrink!" I shouted. "What a dirty trick!" I started to back away, but my father grabbed me by the arm.

"Just talk to him one time, Charlie," he said. "He can help you feel better. I know he can. If you don't want to come back after that, you won't have to."

Quickly, he pushed open the door. The secretary at the desk looked up and smiled.

"Good morning, Mr. Hickle," she said cheerfully. "This must be Charles."

My father smiled. "Is Dr. Girard ready to see him?" he asked.

"Yes," she answered. "He can go right in."

My father opened the door to the next office and gave me a shove. "I'll be right out here if you need me," he said.

I saw Dr. Girard sitting at his desk. He wasn't very old. And when he stood up to greet me, I could see that he was wearing blue jeans. I don't know why, but that really surprised me. I didn't think that grownups were allowed to wear jeans to work.

"Hi, Charlie," he said, smiling. "I'm Henry Girard."

I didn't smile. As a matter of fact, I didn't even say hello. I just sort of stood there feeling like a fool. I still couldn't believe that I was talking to a child psychologist. It made me feel very spooky. Like I was ready for the nut house or something.

"Please sit down," said Dr. Girard.

I sat.

"Do you know why your father brought you here today?" he asked.

"Not unless you happen to serve breakfast," I answered. "I thought he was taking me out to breakfast."

"No, Charlie," he said, laughing out loud. "I even have a hard time trying to make a bowl of cereal."

"That's what I was afraid of," I said.

"Believe me," said Dr. Girard. "There's nothing to be worried about. Your dad just brought you here today because he thinks that you're very unhappy. And he was hoping that maybe I could help you feel a little better. That's all."

I just sat there. I didn't know what I was supposed to say. I had never been crazy before.

"Do you want to tell me about it?" he asked.

"No thanks," I said.

I wasn't really trying to be rude. But I felt really

62

weird sitting there talking to some strange man I didn't even know. Parents can really mix you up. All your life, they go around telling you not to talk to strangers. Then all of a sudden, just because you get a little sad, they dump you in some strange guy's office and tell you to spill your guts out. . . .

"Where's the couch?" I asked finally. "Aren't crazy people supposed to lie down on a couch when they talk to you?"

Dr. Girard laughed. "I don't get many 'crazy' people in here," he said. "But, don't worry, you're not the only one who thinks that you have to be crazy to be here. In fact, at first, almost everyone I see thinks that."

The guy was trying to be understanding, but it didn't help. He was still a stranger.

"It probably feels funny talking to a stranger about your problems, doesn't it?" asked Dr. Girard.

Boy, was that ever a spooky thing to say. It was almost like he could read my mind or something.

I nodded my head. I might as well tell him the truth, I thought. There's not much sense lying to a guy who can read your mind.

"Listen, Charlie," he said. "I promise you, you won't have to tell me anything that you don't want to. All I would like for you to do is answer me one small question. Okay?"

I nodded again.

"Okay," he said. "Here's the question. How do I look?"

God, I thought, what a stupid question! This guy was acting crazier than I was!

I didn't answer. If you ask me, answering a stupid question is just as stupid as asking it. But Dr. Girard just sat there staring at me.

"Come on," he said. "How do I look?"

I was going to try to outstare him, but he was probably a lot better at staring than I was. He got to stare at people all day. So finally I gave in and answered the stupid question.

"You look just fine," I said. "Can I go now?"

Dr. Girard laughed again. For a guy who worked with crazy people all day, he sure did laugh a lot. I would think that crazy people could make you pretty depressed.

"No, Charlie," he said, "I mean do I look happy or sad or mad or angry? How do you think I look?"

I shrugged my shoulders. "I don't know," I said. "I guess you look pretty happy."

"You're right, Charlie," he said. "I am pretty happy."

Goody-goody for you, I thought. Geez! This guy was acting like an idiot. Personally, I didn't care whether he was happy or not. All I wanted to do was get out of there. But, unfortunately, Dr. Girard continued to talk.

"The thing is," he said, "I wasn't always as happy as I am right now. As a matter of fact, Charlie, when I was your age, I was just about the most miserable person that you've ever seen in your life."

64

I knew that he was waiting for me to ask why. And I tried very hard not to. But for some reason I was really curious.

"Okay," I said, "I give up. Why were you miserable?"

"For the exact same reason that you are. And for the same reason that many of the kids that come to see me are. I was miserable because my parents were getting divorced."

I should have known he was going to say that. He was just trying to find a way to get me to talk about my parents. It was very sneaky, but it wouldn't work.

"As a matter of fact," continued Dr. Girard, "I was so unhappy about the divorce, that I did something very very strange."

Once again my curiosity got to me. What in the world could he have done that was any stranger than the things I had done? If he said that he had gone to live in a tree, I would know that he was just making this whole thing up.

"What did you do?" I asked, again.

"I stopped speaking to my parents," he said, acting like it was some big deal.

Geez! What a terrible imagination! Couldn't he make up something better than that?

"No offense, Dr. Girard," I said, "but what's such a big deal about that? I stop speaking to my parents all the time."

"For a whole year?" he asked. "I didn't speak to

either one of my parents for a year. Not one word."

"Oh, come on, Dr. Girard," I said rather angrily. "I'm not some dumb little kid, you know. I know what you're trying to do. You're just trying to get me to talk by making up a bunch of stories."

Dr. Girard leaned way over his desk and looked me straight in the eye.

"One whole year," he said again. Only this time, the way he said it, I knew that he meant it.

"Come on, Dr. Girard," I said. "How could anyone stop talking for a whole year?"

"Wait a minute, Charlie," he said. "I didn't say that I stopped talking. I said that I stopped talking to my *parents*. I talked to everyone else just fine."

By this time, I was sure that he was telling me the truth.

"Wow!" I said, "My mother gets mad at me if I clam up for even a couple of hours! What did your parents do to you?"

"They did just what your father did to you today," he said. "They took me to a psychologist. In fact, they took me to a bunch of psychologists. But it didn't do any good. I was a very stubborn kid."

"You mean you didn't say anything to them at all?" I asked again. "Not even one little peep? Nothing? Never?"

Dr. Girard shook his head. "Nope," he said. "Once in a while, when they asked me a question, I would shake my head yes or no, but that's about it. I never said one word. Not even at Christmas."

"You mean you didn't even ask for any presents?" I asked. This guy was amazing.

"Not one," he said. "And, believe me, that turned out to be a very big mistake."

"Why?" I asked. "What happened?"

"Well," he said, "that Christmas I wanted a basketball hoop and a stereo. But since I wasn't speaking, no one knew it. I thought about writing my list on a piece of paper, but I decided that that would be almost like talking, so I didn't do it.

"Anyway," he continued, "when I got up on Christmas morning, all I found was a game of Monopoly, some clothes, and a stupid pair of mittens with Mickey Mouse on the front of them."

I started laughing.

"Don't laugh," said Dr. Girard. "That's not the worst part. Do you know what I found in my stocking?"

I shook my head no.

"A banana and two pairs of underpants."

I laughed even harder.

"Take it from me, Charlie," he said, smiling, "if you ever decide to stop talking to your parents, don't do it at Christmastime."

"Don't worry," I said, "I could never last as long as you did. I always think of too many mean things that I want to say to them."

Dr. Girard still smiled. "That's okay," he said. "Sometimes it's better to say what's on your mind than to keep it all inside."

"Yeah," I said, "well, saying what's on my mind sure doesn't seem to be helping me much. I still feel just as rotten as I did before. Maybe even rottener . . ."

"Tell me something, Charlie," said Dr. Girard. "When did you first find out that your parents were going to get a divorce?"

"Last Sunday night," I answered.

Dr. Girard looked a little bit surprised. "Charlie," he said, "that's only last week!"

"I know," I said. "And I still feel just as bad now as I did then."

"But what I'm trying to tell you is that a week is a very, very short time," he said. "And if you're planning to feel better already, I'm afraid you're in for a very unpleasant surprise. It takes time to get over something as big as this, Charlie. Lots of it."

"I know, Dr. Girard," I said. "But every day I feel sadder than the day before. Every day I get worse instead of better."

"Okay," said Dr. Girard. "Let me try to explain something to you.

"What if last Sunday night, instead of finding out about the divorce, you had an accident. Let's say, hmm . . . let's say that you took a header off your bicycle. Okay?"

"Okay," I answered.

He continued. "And let's also say that you broke your arm."

"Okay," I said again.

"Well then," he said, "if last Sunday night you took a header off your bicycle and broke your arm, would you expect to be all better by today?"

I shook my head.

"No," he said, "of course you wouldn't. Because you know that broken bones take lots of time to heal. But what a lot of people don't know is that there is another part of us that takes even longer to heal than broken bones. And that is our feelings, Charlie. Hurt, broken feelings. . . ."

"I don't think you understand, Dr. Girard," I said. "It's not just my feelings that are hurt. It's a lot worse than that. Hurt feelings happen when your father puts his chef's hat on his hand instead of his head. I can handle stuff like that. It happens to me all the time."

Dr. Girard looked puzzled. But, I didn't feel like explaining the whole chef's hat thing, so I just kept right on talking.

"My parents are ruining my whole life," I said. "It's all going to change."

"Like what?" asked Dr. Girard.

"Like what?" I asked back. "You ought to know. Like everything, that's what! Like the three of us will never take a vacation together again. And on Christmas morning, it will only be Mom and me. And whenever I have something special to tell my dad, I'll have to call him on the phone. Before, when I had something to tell him, I used to just listen for the sound of his car pulling into the driveway after work. But I can't do that anymore. Because he won't be coming. It's not his home anymore."

"It doesn't seem fair, does it Charlie?" said Dr. Girard. "You're not the one who caused any of this, but you're the one feeling all the hurt."

I hated to admit it, but maybe Dr. Girard understood after all.

I felt tears coming into my eyes. I've always thought it was really embarrassing to cry in front of strangers. You have to keep you head bent way down and hope that your nose doesn't start running. If your nose runs, you've had it. You always end up wiping it on your sleeve. It's really disgusting.

This time, I decided to do something before that happened.

"Do you have a Kleenex, Dr. Girard?" I asked. "I think a bug just flew into my eye."

Dr. Girard handed me a whole box of them off his desk. I blew my nose a couple of times.

"I must be catching a cold," I said.

Dr. Girard didn't say anything. But, I have a feeling that he knew.

"How much time do you think it will take before I feel better?" I asked.

"I won't kid you, Charlie," said Dr. Girard. "It's not going to be quick. But there are certain things that you can do to help speed things along."

"Like what?" I asked.

"Like telling your parents what you're thinking,"

he answered. "And not keeping your feelings all locked up inside of you. Keeping everything in only makes it hurt worse."

"I've already told them a lot of stuff," I said.

"That's good, Charlie," he said. "But just remember. There's a big difference between 'telling' your feelings and 'yelling' your feelings."

I smiled.

Dr. Girard didn't feel like a stranger anymore.

"I've really enjoyed talking to you, Charlie," he said. "I'm here every day, Monday to Friday, plus most Saturdays. If you ever feel like talking again, just give me a call."

When he was finished talking, he got up out of his chair and reached out to shake my hand. Whenever someone shakes my hand, it always makes me feel funny. I never know how hard I'm supposed to squeeze. If you squeeze too tight, the other person always says, "Wow, that's quite a grip you've got there!" God, I hate it when somebody says that.

Anyway, this time I must have squeezed just right. Dr. Girard didn't say anything.

When I left the office, the secretary gave me a card with his number on it. I shoved it in my pocket.

My father came over and put his arm around me.

"How did it go?" he asked, as we walked outside.

At first, I wasn't going to speak to him. But then I thought about what Dr. Girard had said, and decided to really let him have it.

71

"I think it was really rotten for you to bring me here without even telling me," I said, trying not to yell. "At least you could have been honest about it. I thought you were taking me out to breakfast."

I could tell that my father knew I was right.

"I'm sorry, Charles," he said. "I know that I should have told you. But I was afraid if you had known where we were going, you wouldn't have wanted to come."

True. Very true. But I didn't admit it.

"Listen," he said, "It's still not too late for some breakfast. Why don't we go over to my apartment and I'll fix us something."

"No thanks," I said. I couldn't let him off too easy. "I have a hard time eating over there."

My father drove me home without saying another word. When I got there, I went straight to my room. Only this time I didn't cry. Something inside me felt different.

I took out Dr. Girard's card and looked at it. I had to make sure none of my friends ever saw it. Some of them just wouldn't understand. I walked over to my wastebasket and ripped it into a million pieces.

But before I did, I memorized the number.

10

TWO WEEKS after I first met Dr. Girard, it was Easter. But with all the problems that were going on in my family, I had almost forgotten about it.

To tell you the truth, Easter isn't one of my favorite holidays anyway. It's better than nothing, but that's about it.

A lot of holidays seem to lose their fun when you start getting older. Easter is one of them. Halloween is another one. Easter was much better when I was little. I really loved it then.

I guess there are a lot of little kids who never take the Easter Bunny seriously. Let's face it. Trying to believe that there's a giant rabbit hopping all over the world delivering eggs isn't that easy. Personally, I think that it would make a lot more sense if there was an Easter Chicken. But, when I was little, it didn't matter. I was one of those kids who believed whatever my parents told me. If they had told me that there was an Easter Lizard, I would have believed that, too.

When I finally found out that the Easter Bunny was all a big lie, I really took it hard. And, guess who told me? Good old MaryAnn Brady.

She came to school right before Easter vacation, and said her mother had told her the Easter Bunny was just make-believe. She said it was really just your parents. I bet her mother also told her to keep it a secret. But as you can see, even when she was little, MaryAnn was a big blabbo.

When I got home that day, I ran to my mother and asked if what MaryAnn had said was true.

"Is the Easter Bunny real or is it just pretend?" I asked.

My mother stopped what she was doing and looked at me.

"Why?" she asked. "Did someone tell you it wasn't real?"

I nodded.

"MaryAnn Brady," I answered. "She said her mother told her that the Easter Bunny was really your parents."

"Well," said my mother. "Would you really be upset if I told you that the Easter Bunny was Dad and me?"

"No," I answered, "I wouldn't care."

Then she bent down next to me. "Well, then, I guess that means you're old enough to know," she said. "MaryAnn was right. The Easter Bunny really is just Mom and Dad."

"Oh no!" I screamed, "Oh no! Why did you have

to tell me? Oh no! YOU JUST WRECKED MY WHOLE EASTER!"

My mother was very surprised. "But Charlie," she said, "you just told me that you wouldn't care."

"I was only kidding!" I screamed. "I really did care! And now it's all ruined! You spoiled my whole Easter!"

I was a very weird little kid. It took me a week before I finally settled down. And if you think that was bad, you should have seen me when I found out that there wasn't a Santa Claus.

Anyway, ever since then, Easter has lost most of its fun. Once you've looked in your basket and eaten some chocolate, there's nothing much left to do.

My mother knows how I feel about Easter. But for some reason, this year she kept trying to make a big deal out of it. She kept saying stuff like "Only six more days until Easter, Charlie."

"Am I getting a basket this year?" I asked her. I decided I might be getting a little old for that kind of stuff. I wasn't a dumb little kid anymore.

My mother smiled. "Of *course* you're getting one!" she said, misunderstanding completely.

"Well, don't you think I'm getting a little old for a basket?" I said so she'd get the point.

"You'll never be too old for an Easter basket!" my mother chimed. "Never!" And that was that.

On the Saturday before Easter, my mother went to the grocery store. When she came home, she had bought about a million eggs and one of those egg-dyeing kits. I didn't really want to color eggs either, but since she had already bought the stuff, I decided I'd give it a try.

My mother got everything ready and called me. She really seemed excited about the whole thing. When I went into the kitchen, I saw that there were eight cups lined up on the counter. In each cup, there was a different color dye. I decided to get right to it, and get the whole thing over with.

After I had dyed one egg in each color, I started to leave.

"Is that it?" asked my mother. "Is that all you're going to do?"

"I did one in every color," I answered. "How many was I supposed to do?"

My mother went to the refrigerator and pulled out a big bowl. I boiled three dozen eggs, Charles," she said. "You've still got twenty-eight more to go."

Twenty-eight more? Oh, no, I thought. Not twenty-eight more! What in the world were we going to do with all those eggs? I hope my mother didn't think I was going to eat them. Because I think hard-boiled eggs are weird. The yellow part is all dry and pasty, and the white part doesn't have any flavor at all.

"Why did you cook so many?" I asked.

"It's a surprise," she said, winking. "You'll find out tomorrow. Right now, just finish coloring them."

It took me about two hours to finish dyeing all the

eggs. I tried to jazz up a couple of them by putting on some stickers. Every egg-dyeing kit in the world comes with a bunch of dumb-looking stickers. Usually they're pictures of blue baby chicks pushing little wheelbarrows. You've probably seen the kind I mean. They always look real cute on the front of the egg kit. But as soon as you put them on your own eggs, they bunch all up and look awful.

"I'm done," I said, finally. "Is Dad coming over tomorrow? Is that the surprise?"

"No," answered my mother. "Your father's not coming tomorrow. I've got something else planned."

Then she smiled and winked again.

I hate it when my mother winks. It was okay when I was little. Then, I used to try and wink back. But now it just seems silly.

On Easter morning, when I woke up, I have to admit I was pretty excited. It wasn't about the Easter basket, though. I just couldn't wait to see what kind of surprise my mother had planned.

When I got out of bed, I hurried to the kitchen. On the table, I found my Easter basket stuffed full of chocolate bunnies and jellybeans. Just as I thought, it made me feel dumb.

"Where's the big surprise?" I asked my mother after thanking her for the candy.

"It's coming later on in the day," she answered. Then she winked at me again.

"Mom," I said, "there's something I need to tell

you. Dr. Girard said that if something bothers me, I should get it off my chest."

My mother looked very worried. She sat down in the chair next to me. I guess she thought that I was going to talk about the divorce.

"Sure, honey," she said, "tell me what's on your mind."

"I wish you would stop winking at me," I said. "It makes me feel ridiculous."

My mother got up quickly. She didn't say anything. She looked very annoyed.

"I didn't mean to make you mad," I said. "It's just that at my age, winking makes me feel like a fool."

"Fine," said my mother. "I'll never wink again." Then she left the room in a huff. I never realized that winking meant so much to her.

After that, the morning passed pretty slowly. Time always passes slowly when you're waiting for a surprise.

By about two o'clock, I started to wonder if maybe my mother had called off the surprise. I figured maybe she was even madder about the winking than I had thought. But just then, I heard the doorbell.

This must be it! I thought to myself as I ran to the door. Quickly, I pulled it open.

There stood Hank.

Hank is one of my mother's cousins. She has three of them. Two of them are really neat. The other one is Hank.

78

We don't see Hank very often. He lives about fifty miles away. I think it's what I like best about him.

Hank's a real cornball. You can tell he doesn't have any kids of his own. He's always saying the kind of stuff kids hate, you know, like calling you "little man" and junk like that.

When I saw him standing there, I guess I must have looked pretty surprised. I just sort of stared at him for a minute.

Hank pushed his way into the house. "Hi ya there, Chas!" he said loudly. As soon as he got in, he picked me up and swung me around.

I hate being swung around almost as much as I hate being called Chas.

Finally, Hank put me down and stuck out his hand. "Put 'er there, big guy," he said, waiting for me to shake it.

I shook it.

"OOOOIIIEEEE!" he hollered, rubbing his hand as I let go. "THAT'S REALLY SOME GRIP YOU'VE GOT THERE, TIGER!"

"I'll get Mom for you," I said a little disgustedly. Then I turned and ran full speed ahead to my mother's room.

I hoped she wouldn't be too upset. She usually doesn't like it when company drops by unexpectedly.

When I ran in, she had just finished combing her hair.

"Mom!" I said excitedly, "You're not going to believe this! But your cousin Hank just showed up at the front door! He's standing out there in the hall waiting for you!"

My mother was very calm. "I know," she said, smiling.

"Whew!" I said, "That's a relief! I thought he had just dropped by or something."

"No," she said. "I knew he was coming."

"Well, you better get out there," I said. "I'm going to be in my room for a while. Call me when the surprise gets here, okay?"

My mother's face went all funny.

"What did you say?" she asked.

"I said 'Call me when the surprise gets here,'" I repeated.

My mother just stared at me. "Charlie," she said finally, "Cousin Hank *is* the surprise. . . ."

I was hoping I hadn't heard her right.

"Hank?" I asked. "Hank is the big surprise?"

"Yes," she answered. "I called him to spend Easter with us."

"Why?" I asked, puzzled.

"Well, I just thought it would be nice if we had someone over here to share our Easter dinner with us."

"Why?" I asked again.

"Well, I just didn't want you to feel lonely on Easter, that's all," she said.

80

"Oh," I said. I guess I should have tried to act happier, but "why" and "oh" seemed to be the only two things that would come out of my mouth.

Mother put her arm on my shoulder and we walked back to the hall. Hank was still there. My mother started to hug him. He picked her up and swung her around. Then the three of us went into the living room and sat down.

"Did you get the eggs ready for us?" asked Hank.

My mother nodded. "Charlie did them all himself," she said.

Then she turned to me. "Hank had this great idea, Charles," she said. "We're going to send you on an Easter-egg hunt. That's what all the eggs were for."

"Oh," I said again.

"When I was a boy," said Hank, "my parents always hid eggs in the backyard. Then my brother and I would go out and try to find them. The best thing about it was that my dad gave us a penny for every egg we found."

"Oh," I said, for the third time.

"Well," said my mother, "doesn't that sound like fun?"

Dumb. It sounded dumb. But I didn't want to hurt my mother's feelings.

I forced myself to nod my head. "Fun," I said. "Fun."

Hank stood up and headed for the backyard.

"You'll only have five minutes to find them," he giggled. "And I'll give you a nickel for every one you find!"

Oh, whoopee, I thought to myself.

"You stay here now, Charlie," said my mother. "Hank and I will go hide the eggs. And remember . . . no peeking!"

The two of them hurried outside. Meanwhile, I waited alone in the living room.

After a few minutes had passed, Hank called me from the back door. "OKAY, CHAS!" he shouted. "YOU CAN COME NOW! WE'RE READY!"

Slowly, I got up and walked outside. Believe me, I was in no hurry. This was one of the dumbest things I'd ever had to do in my life.

When I got outside, my mother and Hank were standing there grinning. It was obvious that they were having a lot better time than I was.

"Okay, Chas," said Hank, "you've got five minutes."

My mother shoved an empty basket in my hand. "Ten-nine-eight-seven-six-five-four-three-two-one. GO!" she shouted.

I couldn't stand how stupid she was acting.

"God, Mother," I said. "I'm not a rocket ship!"

My mother hates it when I say "God." But saying "God" is as close as I can get to really swearing, without getting punished. So sometimes I say it anyway.

This time, she ignored me.

82

"GO! GO!" she yelled again. "Start looking!"

Hank started clapping his hands. "Hurry up, Chas," he said, "you've already wasted forty seconds."

I walked out into the middle of the yard and looked around. I spotted three eggs in the bushes. They were lying out in plain sight. Hank must have thought I needed glasses or something.

I picked them up and put them in my basket. I looked around and saw a couple more around the tree. I walked over and gathered them up. Two more were balanced in the branches. I grabbed them also.

So far I had collected seven eggs. There were twenty-nine more to go. I made my way around the yard picking up the eggs as I walked along. Not one of them was hard to find.

Finally, Hank shouted for me to stop. "TIME'S UP!" he roared. "Bring your basket in!"

I wished he hadn't shouted so loud. If any of my friends knew that I was hunting for eggs, I would have died. Slowly I carried the basket over to the patio. My mother quickly counted them.

"Thirty-six!" she said. "That's great, Charlie! You found every single one of them!!!"

"Shh," I said. "Not so loud."

Hank laughed. "You should be proud of yourself!" he said. "When my brother and I used to do this, we never found all of them!"

"Maybe your parents didn't put them out in plain

sight," I said. "I tripped over three of them."

Hank laughed again. "Let's see now," he said, reaching into his pocket. "How much does old cousin Hank owe you?"

"A dollar eighty," I said quickly. I had added the whole thing up before I ever started. If you're going to make a fool out of yourself, you ought to be sure it's worth it.

Hank handed me the money.

"Thanks," I said.

I turned to my mother. "Is this the end of the 'fun'?" I asked. "Would it be all right if I went in now?"

"Go ahead," she said. "Dinner will be ready in a few minutes."

I went inside and turned on the TV. Naturally nothing was on. I've decided that all television stations save their worst shows for Sunday afternoon. They must figure that on Sunday afternoon people are so bored they'll watch anything.

They're right. I started watching this real boring show about how to fix up your old furniture.

My mother and Hank stayed outside and talked for a few minutes. When my mother came in to fix dinner, Hank plopped himself beside me on the couch.

"What'cha watchin', big guy?" he asked.

I can't decide which I hate worse, "Chas" or "big guy."

"Nothing much," I answered. "Just a dumb show."

"You mind if cousin Hank watches it with you?" he asked again.

I managed to shake my head no. But it wasn't easy. I minded a lot. The guy was really getting on my nerves. I thought if he called me Chas one more time, I would blow up.

"What's this show about, Chas?" he asked then.

Quickly, I sprung up from the couch. "Stop calling me Chas!" I hollered. "I hate it! How would you like me to call you Hanky? Would you like to be called Hanky?"

Hank didn't do anything for a minute. He just sat there looking at me. His face looked a little confused. But mostly, it just looked sad.

"I'm sorry," he said finally. "I didn't know."

Right away I felt terrible. I knew I shouldn't have shouted at him like that. But it just seemed like everything was going wrong.

My mother had heard me yelling. She came in and grabbed me by the arm.

"Will you please excuse us for a minute, Hank?" she asked. But she didn't wait for an answer. She just pulled me down the hall to my room.

"How could you have done that?" she said, closing my door. "How could you be so mean?"

I didn't know myself, so I couldn't answer.

"What kind of kid are you, anyway?" she contin-

85

ued. "Here poor Hank drives all this way to spend Easter with you, and you stand there and scream at him! How could you, Charlie? How could you?"

I shrugged my shoulders.

"I don't know," I said, finally. "I didn't mean to." I felt a couple of tears creeping into my eyes. "It's just that I didn't really expect Hank to be the surprise, I guess."

"Oh, well, that's just wonderful," said my mother. "Now what am I supposed to do . . . tell him he wasn't a good enough surprise and send him home? Or first, maybe you'd like to yell at him some more."

Boy! Was she ever mad!

"I'm sorry," I said. "I didn't mean it."

"Well, don't tell me," said my mother. "I'm not the one who drove fifty miles to spend Easter with you. If you're sorry, go tell Hank."

I knew she was going to tell me to apologize. My mother is real big on apologizing. Especially when it's me doing it.

But this time, I knew she was right. I knew it as soon as I saw how bad my words had made Hank feel.

I walked back into the living room. Hank was sitting there pretending to watch the furniture show.

"Hank," I said nervously, "I'm sorry for yelling at you like that. I didn't mean to make you feel bad. Honest."

Hank smiled. "That's okay, Charles," he said. "Don't worry about it. I guess we all have to yell once in a while."

"You can call me Charlie," I said, trying to smile.

Hank reached over and rumpled my hair. (Ugh!)

"Okay, big guy," he said.

About that time, my mother called us for dinner. While we were eating, no one said very much. I tried to smile a lot to make up for it. So did my mother and Hank. Sometimes it takes a while for people to act normal after there's been an argument.

After dinner, Hank stuck around for a couple of hours. He still acted corny, but for some reason I didn't mind it as much. I guess just because someone is a big cornball, that's no reason not to like him.

I just hope that my mother doesn't think she needs to call Hank every time there's a holiday. If I thought his Easter-egg hunt was dumb, I'd hate to see what he'd come up with for Halloween.

Thinking about this made me very nervous. I wanted to tell my mother how I felt, but I was afraid she would get mad at me all over again. I suddenly wondered what Dr. Girard would have done if he were me. There was only one way to find out.

I headed for the phone and dialed his number.

The voice on the other end was a recording. It said: "Dr. Girard is not in the office right now. At the sound of the beep, please leave your name and telephone number, and Dr. Girard will return your call. . . . Beep!"

"This is Charles Hickle," I said nervously. "My number is 555-6788."

After I hung up, I felt much better. Just knowing there's someone to talk to really helped.

SO FAR, I've talked to Dr. Girard three times. And each time he makes me feel a little bit better about things. At least I don't want to live in a tree as much as I did before.

Don't get me wrong, though. I still don't think I'm ever going to get over this. And, I still think divorce is a stinko thing for parents to do.

It's really hard for me to get used to living just with my mother. It must be weird for her, too. Almost every night, when she sets the table, she puts on three plates.

Once in a while, my mother calls me "the man of the house." I don't know if she's trying to make me feel grown-up or what. Just because they decided to get divorced doesn't suddenly turn me into a man. I don't even shave yet. The next thing you know, she'll expect me to go to work, or something.

Of course, maybe work wouldn't be so bad. It's got to be better than school. Because, to tell you the truth, school hasn't been going well for me at all lately. I used to be pretty good in school, but ever since the divorce, I've really had a hard time keeping my mind on stuff. Somehow, learning how brine shrimp lay eggs just doesn't seem important.

Right after my teacher found out that things were bad for me at home, she got real nice. She hardly made me do any work at all. But teachers don't stay real nice like that for very long. I think it's one of the rules of being a teacher.

Anyway, last Friday after school, Mrs. Fensel handed me a note to take home to my mother. She told me to be sure to show it to her.

"I'm going to trust you not to read it, Charles," she said.

Well, that was a big fat lie. If she "trusted me not to read it," why did she have it all sealed up with tape? Does that sound like "trust" to you?

Having to take a note home to your mother is probably one of the worst things a kid ever has to do. Carrying it gives you this real sick feeling inside. It's a lot like asking a criminal to cut off his own head. It's just not fair.

All the way home I kept waiting for a big strong gust of wind to come along and blow the note out of my hand. I just laid it in my palm and waited. But as usual, there's never a good wind when you need one. Never.

The same thing happens whenever I want to fly my kite. I spend about an hour untangling my ball of string. And by the time I finally get ready to fly the darn thing, the wind's stopped. So I end up dragging it up and down the street a couple of times and putting it away.

The only time it's ever windy is when you don't want it to be. Like when you finish swimming. I don't know where the wind comes from, but as soon as you get out of the water, a big gust always comes along and freezes your tail off.

Anyway, the day Mrs. Fensel gave me the note, the wind was nowhere to be found. I tried blowing on it myself. I figured if I blew it away myself, I would still be able to tell my mother that the wind got it.

But it didn't work. I think all the tape was weighing it down.

When I got home, I didn't give the note to my mother right away. I decided to take it into my room first. I thought that maybe I could hold it up to the light and read it. But, when I tried to, all I could see was that the note was folded into a tiny little wad. Boy, that old Mrs. Fensel really thought of everything.

The funny thing was, I really didn't need to read the note at all. I knew exactly what it was going to say. And if I was right, my mother wasn't going to be too thrilled about it.

Lately my papers haven't been too good. The highest mark I've received in the past few weeks has been a D+. I got it in spelling. I would have gotten a C−, but I forgot to capitalize *Russia*.

Personally, I think it's really stupid to count a word wrong just because you didn't use a capital. It's not that you're using the wrong letter, it's just that you've used it in a different size.

Before I took the note out to my mother, I began to think about how much trouble I was going to be in. And for the first time in five weeks, I began to think about living in a tree again. When it comes to getting good grades, my mother is really tough.

I knew exactly what she was going to do. She would read the note and then call me into the living room for a little "talk." And if there's one thing that I hate, it's my mother's little "talks."

She starts out by telling me how she isn't going to yell or scold me. Then she yells and scolds me. After that, she takes away all the fun things that I like to do, and tries to make it seem like it's for "my own good." She likes to make *all* the mean things she does seem like they're "for my own good." That way, she doesn't feel like such a creep.

The more I thought about this, the dumber it seemed to give her the note. After all, if I already knew what she was going to say, there wasn't any point in making her upset about it. All I had to do was save her the trouble of punishing me. So I decided to stop watching as much TV at night and study harder.

There! I said to myself. Now my poor mother won't have to feel like a creep. She has enough on her mind without adding that to her problems.

Besides, Mrs. Fensel hadn't really told me to "give" my mother the note. She just asked me to "show" it to her. So as long as I "showed" it to her, I really wouldn't be doing anything wrong.

I heard my mother banging around in the kitchen. I took the note out of my back pocket and went in to say hello.

Then, after I had talked to her for a couple of minutes, I pulled the note out of my pocket and dropped it on the floor.

"What's that?" asked my mother.

"Oh, it's just a note that someone wrote at school," I answered.

My mother started to grin.

"Ohhhhh . . . I see," she said. "Got yourself a secret admirer, huh?"

I just smiled back and left the kitchen. When I got back to my room I felt much better. "There!" I said, right out loud. "Now I won't be lying when I tell Mrs. Fensel that my mother "saw" the note. There's no doubt about it. I am definitely a very clever kid.

Now that that was over with, there really wasn't any reason why I couldn't open the note and read it. No one would ever know, and I was really dying to see what kind of mean stuff Mrs. Fensel had written about me.

I tried to tear open the envelope with my hands, but it wouldn't budge. "Is this what you call trust, Mrs. Fensel, you old bat?" I said. Then I laughed.

Finally, I managed to slit open the bottom of the envelope with my pen. I pulled the note out, and began reading. . . .

Dear Mrs. Hickle,

This note is to let you know that your son, Charles, has been doing very poorly with his schoolwork. In the past month, Charles has had no grade higher than a D+.

Mrs. Hickle, I do understand that Charles has been having some problems at home, and I have tried to be understanding. But he does not seem to be getting any better, so I feel it's time I let you know what is happening.

In addition to his grades, his behavior has also taken a turn for the worse. Charles used to be a very well-behaved boy. Lately, however, he has started to become rather rude, both to me and to others in the classroom.

I would appreciate any effort that you and his father would take to see that Charles changes both his behavior and his grades. Maybe if you and I can work together, we will be able to get him back on the right track.

Sincerely,
Edna Fensel

I couldn't believe it! Rude! She actually told my mother that I was RUDE!

What's so rude about telling a teacher that spelling stinks? Especially when she asks you! And especially when it's the truth! Besides, Mrs. Fensel started the whole thing herself.

After I got my last spelling test back, she came over to my desk and asked me what was wrong with my spelling lately.

"Nothing is wrong with my spelling," I said. "The reason I got a D is because you marked "russia" wrong. I spelled "russia" right."

She looked at my paper.

"*Russia* has a capital," she said.

"I know," I said. "The capital of Russia is Moscow."

Mrs. Fensel didn't laugh at my joke. She pretended she didn't even hear it.

"If you don't spell it with a capital, it's wrong," she said.

That's when I said, "Spelling stinks."

"Excuse me?" said Mrs. Fensel, sounding very annoyed.

"Stinks. S–T–I–N–K–S," I spelled.

Mrs. Fensel shook her head and walked away. At first, I didn't think she was going to do anything. But, I guess I was wrong. Because, instead of yelling at me, she wrote that note to my mother. What a tattletale! A guy spells one lousy *stinks* and boom . . . he gets a note sent home.

Anyway, after I read it, I was very glad I hadn't shown my mother the note. At least I was glad until about 8:30. At 8:30, I stopped being glad. That's when Mrs. Fensel called.

I was in the shower when the phone rang. But after I got out, I could hear my mother talking. And, it didn't take long to figure out who she was talking to. She kept saying stuff like, "Yes, Mrs. Fensel, I know he's having a hard time." And, "no, Mrs. Fensel, I don't know why he didn't show it to me."

I was doomed. Doomed. Doomed. Doomed.

Or was I?

An idea popped into my head. I threw on my pajamas and dashed into my room to get the note. I decided not to put it back in its torn-up envelope. I thought it might look suspicious. So, I just folded it up and ran to my mother. She had just hung up the phone.

"Oh my gosh, Mom!" I shouted. "I almost forgot to give you this note! I just thought about it while I was in the shower! It's from Mrs. Fensel."

My mother grabbed the note out of my hand and read it. She had this look on her face like she was about to explode.

After she finished reading, her expression changed. She got this real funny grin on her face. But, it wasn't exactly what you'd call a happy grin. It was more like the kind of grin that crazy people have on TV.

She started walking toward me very slowly. It really got me scared. I started backing up. I backed into the wall. She had me cornered.

My mother got real close to me. Then she reached out, put her hands on my shoulders, and began talking very quietly. She still had that spooky grin on her face.

"Charles," she said. "I'm going to give you exactly three weeks. That's three," she repeated as she held up her fingers. "One . . . two . . . three. And if, at the end of three weeks, your grades aren't back up to where they are supposed to be, you are going to be a very unhappy boy."

I looked at her face. That grin was making me very nervous.

"What do you mean?" I gulped. "What will happen to me?"

"Try me, Charles," she said, still smiling. "Just try me."

"Well, ah, couldn't you just give me a little hint?" I asked nervously.

"A little hint?" she repeated. "Sure, okay. . . . I'll give you lots of little hints.

"Hmmm, let's see. . . . Okay, little hint number one, no TV. Little hint number two, no sports. Little hint number three, no friends. Little hint number four, no telephone. Little hint number five, no record player. Little hint number six, no radio. Little hint number seven, no allowance. . . . Are you getting the picture yet, Charles?" she asked.

"I don't understand little hint number seven," I said. "I mean I understand no TV and stuff, because I know that I have to study. But, what does my allowance have to do with my schoolwork?"

I wasn't trying to be a smart aleck or anything. I really wanted to know. And my mother made it very clear.

"You won't need any money," she shouted, "because you won't ever be setting foot out of your room to buy anything, because little hint number eight is staying in your room! Got it?"

"Got it," I said, quietly. "Can I go now?"

"Just one more teensy-weensy little thing," said my mother. "If I ever again hear that you've been rude to your teacher, I will personally take you by the hand and lead you to your classroom, where you will stand in the front of the room and apologize to Mrs. Fensel in front of the entire class. DO YOU GET THAT, TOO?"

I nodded. This was definitely something that my mother would do. Like I said before, she's very big on apologizing.

I remember when I was little, I called this old lady down the street an old bag. At the time, I wasn't really sure what an "old bag" was, but I was trying to make some kids laugh, so when we went by her house, I said, "Hi, there, you old bag."

The lady found out who I was and called my mother. The next day, my mother took me down there and made me tell the "old bag" I was sorry for calling her names.

Anyway, I could just see my mother leading me into my classroom and making me tell Mrs. Fensel I was sorry for spelling *stinks*. She'd love it.

98

"Are you going to tell Dad about this?" I asked. "Because, well, ah . . . I was just thinking . . . maybe we could just keep all of this . . . our own little secret. I mean, really . . . there's no need bothering Dad with it, is there? After all, he's got his own problems trying to live in that stinky apartment and everything. What do you say, Mom? Is it a deal?"

My mother didn't hear me. She was already on the phone calling my father.

12

YESTERDAY WAS my eleventh birthday. I wish I had a chance to do it over again. I really blew it. In fact, it was the worst birthday I've ever had in my life. It was even worse than the one when I asked for a real-bow-and-arrow set, and instead got the kind with the rubber suction cups on the ends.

It wasn't the presents that made my birthday rotten. After all, I got exactly what I asked for. I just wish I had asked for something else.

I must admit, though, my mother tried to talk me out of it. It's just that when I started all my begging, I finally made her give in. Sometimes, I wish my mother was a little bit stronger a person.

A week before my birthday, I cornered her in the kitchen.

"Isn't it about time you started thinking about my birthday?" I asked.

My mother got this real serious look on her face.

"You're right," she said. Then she sat down in the kitchen chair and put her head down on the table.

After about thirty seconds had passed, she raised up.

"Okay, I'm finished thinking about it," she said. "Can I get up now?"

"That's not funny," I said, trying to keep from smiling. "Aren't you even going to find out what I want?"

She walked over and put her hands on my shoulders.

"I haven't let you down yet, have I?" she asked.

"How about the time you gave me the arrows with the rubber suction cups on the ends," I reminded her.

"Oh, yeah," she said, laughing. "Okay. You win. What do you want for your birthday?"

I took a deep breath. I had known what I wanted ever since my Dad left. I had a feeling she wasn't going to like the idea. But there was only one way to find out.

"I want to go on a picnic with you and Dad," I said. Then I held my ears and got ready for her to yell.

But instead of yelling, my mother surprised me. She smiled.

"I was expecting you to say something like that," she said.

"Does that mean we can do it?" I asked happily.

"Of course we can't do it," she answered. "Now, how about one of those electronic sports games?"

"I want a picnic!" I insisted. "Just a simple little

picnic. Is that too much to ask? Can't you and Dad just do me this one little favor and take your poor little lonely son on a picnic? I think it's the least you can do. After all, you are ruining my life, you know. I really don't think that one crummy little picnic will kill you."

"Let's compromise," said my mother. "I'll let you eat your birthday cake in the backyard on a blanket."

Then she laughed.

"That's not funny," I said, annoyed.

"Neither is the thought of going on a picnic with your father," she said. "Believe me, Charles, he won't like the idea any better than I do."

"What if I ask him and he says yes?" I asked. "If Dad says he'll go, will you go too?"

"He's *not* going to say yes, Charlie," she answered.

"But, if he does, will you go?" I repeated.

My mother thought about it for a minute.

"Oh, all right," she said, finally, "I'll go if your father goes. But the only reason I'm agreeing to it is because I'm positive that he'll never say yes. I know your father pretty well, Charlie. You can't live with someone for this many years and not know them."

Maybe that was one of my parents' big problems. Maybe they didn't know each other like they thought they did. My father said yes. In fact, he even acted happy about it.

When I asked him if he wanted to go, he got this

big grin on his face. "Sure I'll go," he said. "I can't wait!"

"Mom said you wouldn't want to go," I told him. "In fact, she said that she was positive that you'd hate the idea."

"That's ridiculous," said my dad. "There is no reason in the world why we can't take you on a picnic for your birthday. After all, your mother and I are two grown-up people. We don't go around fighting like a couple of little kids. I'm sure we can still all have a nice time together. Tell her I'll pick you up at 12:00 on Saturday."

I had a feeling that the real reason Dad wanted to go on a picnic was just to get some fresh air. I was sure that by now, the apartment stink had really started to get to him. But, it didn't matter to me why he wanted to go. All I knew was that the three of us would be together again.

"Dad's going to go! He's going to go!" I shouted as I walked in the house. "He thought the picnic was a great idea!"

You should have seen my mother's face when she heard the news. It got this funny look on it, like she had just eaten something that tasted bad.

"Are you sure he knows that I'm going, too?" she asked.

"Positive," I answered, "and he said that you're both adults and you should be able to have a nice time together. He also said that he'd pick us up at 12:00 on Saturday."

"Whoopee," said my mother, "I can hardly wait."

Only it wasn't a happy "Whoopee." It was a real disgusted "whoopee."

By the time Saturday came, I had really started to get excited. I kept hoping that maybe, if we all had a really fun time together, my parents would see what a terrible mistake they were making. I had this idea, that after the picnic, everything would be the same as it always was. We would be a family again.

I was also hoping that my mother really didn't think I meant it when I said *all* I wanted was a picnic. I wanted presents, too. This may sound kind of greedy, but let's face it, your birthday only comes once a year.

When my father came to pick us up, my mother opened the car door to let me in. But, instead of getting in, I bent down and pretended to tie my shoe. My mother stood there for a minute and then got in. Just as she was about to close the door, I grabbed it and said, "Slide over. I don't want to sit in the back." She only moved over about an inch. I had to push her the rest of the way to make room. At first this made me very happy. I thought that maybe if they sat together, they would begin to get that old "married" feeling again. But it didn't work.

They didn't even smile at each other or say hello. All my mother did was keep squeezing over toward my side of the seat, making me real uncomfortable. Every time we went over a bump, the picnic basket poked into my side. Luckily, the park wasn't too far away.

When we got there, I grabbed the blanket from the trunk and ran to find us a perfect spot to sit down. I decided on a place right next to the lake. It was really a pretty spot.

As soon as my parents caught up with me, my mother plopped down on the blanket and started opening up the basket of food.

"Wait a minute," I said. "We're not supposed to eat yet! Usually we play Frisbee or something for a while to work up an appetite."

"I hate to play Frisbee," said my mother. "I always break my fingernails when I catch it."

"How could you break your nails?" laughed my father. "You never catch it!"

"I do too," she answered. "The only time I don't catch it, is when you whiz it at me at ninety miles an hour."

"Oh, don't be such a sissy," said Dad. "Come on, let's play."

My mother stood up. But she was still grumbling.

"Frisbee." she said. "Even the name of it sounds dumb."

The three of us got in a circle. My father tossed the Frisbee to me first. I caught it and threw it back to him.

Next he threw it to my mother. It hit her in the head.

"Ow!" she yelled. "That's it! I'm not playing anymore!"

She stomped over to the blanket and sat back down. I hadn't seen her that mad since I showed her the note from Mrs. Fensel.

She started pulling all the food out of the picnic basket.

"It's time to eat," she shouted. "If you don't come now, the flies will get it."

I went over and bent down next to her. "You're not acting very grown-up about this, Mom," I whispered in her ear.

She told me to shut up. Like I said, she was really mad. There ought to be a law against telling someone to shut up on his birthday.

My father sat down and grabbed a sandwich. "What kind is it?" he asked as he took a big bite.

"Liverwurst," answered my mother, smiling.

"Liverwurst?" he said. "I hate liverwurst!"

"I know," said my mother, smiling even bigger than before.

Things weren't going at all like I had hoped. In fact, I didn't think they could get any worse . . . but, I was wrong.

While we were eating, I noticed this big fat lady walking toward us, carrying a blanket. When she got about three feet from us, she smiled and spread her blanket right next to ours.

I couldn't believe it! The whole park was practically empty, and she has to flop her fat right next to us! But that's not even the worst part. The worst part is that she had her three fat children with her!

And, after a couple of minutes, they came waddling over and flopped down right beside her. Then all four of them sat on their blanket and stared at us.

My mother tried to ignore them, but, believe me, it wasn't easy. They were the rudest kids I had ever seen! I hate being stared at!

At first, I tried staring back, but, it didn't work. The fat kids were much better starers than I was. I always ended up being the first one to look away.

After we had finished eating, my father went to the car and came back with an armful of presents. God! You should have seen the fat kids then! They started to act like they were at my birthday party or something!"

The big fat mother did too. She leaned over and said, "Ooooo. Are you a birthday boy today?"

God! How embarrassing! She actually called me "a birthday boy!" Then, one of the kids pointed to one of my presents and said, "I bet that's a football. Look how it's wrapped. You can tell."

I could tell this made my father mad. It was his present. He'd wrapped it himself. He turned around and told the kid to "please be quiet."

Before I started unwrapping everything, my mother passed out cupcakes to my father and me. As soon as she did that, this real little baby fat kid walked right over on our blanket and said, "Me want cupcake, too."

The fat mother laughed. My mother didn't.

107

"I don't have any more," she said, sounding real grouchy.

"Me want cupcake. Me want cupcake!" screamed the kid again.

"Go on," said my mother. "You look like you've had too many cupcakes already."

When she heard that, the fat lady stopped laughing.

"He's just a baby," she said.

Meanwhile, the kid was still screaming. "Barney want cupcake. Barney want cupcake!"

By this time my mother had really had it. She leaned way over real close to the little fat kid's face and shouted, "No! No cupcake!"

I guess she must have scared him. The kid jumped about a foot and fell over our picnic basket. Then, he started crying as loud as he could.

The fat lady came over and picked him up. She carried him over to her blanket.

"It's people like you who make children afraid of strangers," she said angrily. Then she picked up her blanket and stomped off. Two of the fat kids followed her. One of them just stood there staring at my mother.

"You big meanie!" he said finally.

My mother was even angrier than I had first thought. I could hardly believe what she said next.

"GO HOME, FATTY!" she yelled.

The kid turned and ran.

I still can't believe she did that. Let's face it, "Go

home, fatty," is not something that mothers usually say.

My father and I both just sat there staring at her.

"Well, I'm sorry," said my mother, "but, he was getting on my nerves."

"For heaven's sake," said my father, "he was just a little kid."

"Little?" said my mother. "You call that little? I've seen smaller elephants!"

"You know what I mean," said my dad.

"Well, I said I was sorry," repeated my mother. "So let's just forget it."

Then she turned to me. "Well, are you going to open up your presents or not?"

"Yeah, sure," I answered.

"Which one do you want to open first?" asked my father.

"The football," I said.

My father handed me the package. I could tell he was still mad about it.

"How do you know it's a football?" he said. "Just because that kid said so doesn't mean it's really a football!"

I opened it up.

It was a football.

I opened up the rest of the presents. My mother had bought me an electronic baseball game and a transistor radio. My father gave me a remote-control car.

No one gave me batteries.

After I had thanked them, we all piled in the car and my father drove us home. This time, I sat in the middle. It was much more comfortable that way.

When we got home, my mother and I got out of the car. I started to walk around to say good-bye to my father. But as it turned out, I didn't have to. He was already out of the car and on his way to the house. I guess he just didn't want to leave me on my birthday.

I have to admit, when I saw him going in the front door, it really surprised me. But it must have surprised my mother even more. Before she knew what was happening, he had marched right in and plopped himself down on the couch.

My mother stood there for a minute just staring at him. Finally, she spoke.

"Won't you sit down?" she asked disgustedly.

My father didn't say a word. He just smiled.

This whole thing was beginning to make me very nervous. Having them together at the picnic had turned out to be bad enough. But inside the house was even worse. I knew that sooner or later another argument was going to get started.

I wasn't quite sure what I should do. So finally I just walked over to the couch and sat down next to my dad.

My mother didn't know what to do either. For a while she walked around trying to pretend she was busy. But finally she gave up, and sat down in the chair across from us.

110

For a long time, no one said a word. We all just sat there staring at the floor, waiting for the argument to start. All I could hear was the sound of my father's watch ticking. Tick-tick-tick. . . .

It reminded me of this TV show I saw one time. It was about these two policemen who had to take the fuse out of a time bomb so it wouldn't explode. It really got scary. They had to work very slowly so they wouldn't set it off. The whole time they were working, all you could hear was the tick-tick-tick of the time bomb . . . just like my father's watch.

Finally, I just couldn't stand the silence anymore. I had to do something. I decided to try to start a nice friendly conversation.

"Well," I began, "did you guys have a nice time today?" As it turned out, this was probably the worst question I could have asked.

My father answered first.

"I did," he said. "it was really fun, wasn't it? Especially throwing that old Frisbee around. . . ."

My mother shot him a very dirty look. I heard her mumbling.

"What did you say?" I asked.

"Liverwurst," she repeated. "I said my favorite part of the picnic was the liverwurst."

That did it!

"Excuse me," I said. "I've got to go to the bathroom."

I hurried out of the room and down the hall. As soon as I was out of sight, I ducked into my mother's bedroom and called Dr. Girard.

His secretary said he was busy on the other phone.

"This is an emergency!" I said in my loudest whisper.

Dr. Girard picked up the phone right away.

Quickly I told him what was going on. Twice I almost started to cry.

Dr. Girard and I didn't talk long. We didn't have to. The answer to my problem turned out to be so simple, it's funny I didn't think of it sooner. . . .

When I got off the phone, I rushed into the bathroom and flushed the toilet. Then I went back into the living room and sat back down on the couch next to my father. Only this time, I sat extra close.

"I need to tell you something private," I said quietly.

My father nodded and leaned his head over in my direction.

I cupped my hands around his ear.

"Could you please go home?" I whispered.

My father looked at me and smiled. I knew he would understand.

He got up and said good-bye to my mother. Then I walked him to the door.

When we got there, he bent down and gave me a hug.

"I guess sometimes adults just aren't quite as grown-up as they think they are," he said.

Then he hugged me again and left.

13

TODAY IS SUNDAY. Dad just called. He's going to stop by later on and pick me up. We're going over to his place and toss around my new football.

I don't mind going over there quite as much anymore. He painted the walls and bought himself a new chair to replace the smelly one.

For a joke, he bought me a can of rose-scented bathroom spray. He lets me spray the couch before I sit down.

It's funny, but sometimes, he doesn't seem as much like my father as he used to. Sometimes he seems like more of a friend. . . .

My mother still seems like my mother. But maybe that will be changing, too. The other day she told me that she's looking for a job.

When I first heard her say it, I started laughing. I think I hurt her feelings. I didn't mean to. It's just that she's been a mother so long, it's hard for me to think of her as a regular person.

I talked to Dr. Girard about it. He told me that

when his parents got divorced, his mother became a mailman.

When he said that, I must have laughed for ten minutes. The thought of my mother becoming a mailman really kills me.

That Dr. Girard is a pretty funny guy.

Sometimes I think back to when I first met him. It seems like a long time ago, but it's only been two months.

I think I've come a long way in two months. I don't go around singing all the time, but I don't cry as much either.

I guess nothing can keep you sad forever. Forever is just too long.

It's like that bicycle I talked about earlier. As you stand there and watch it get run over, you get this real sick feeling inside. But after a while, you realize that if you save your money, you can get a new one. It may take some time, but you can do it.

And, even though the second bike may be different from the first one, you can still be happy with it. Just because it's different doesn't make it bad.

I guess that's what I'm trying to do now. I'm trying to be happy with something different. I know it's going to take time before I feel like my old self again. But at least I think I'm making progress.

Take today for instance. . . . When I walked by my mirror this morning, I caught myself smiling. And no one even had to ask.

BARBARA PARK was born and raised in Mount Holly, New Jersey. A graduate of the University of Alabama, she holds a B.S. in education. Barbara and her husband, Richard, now live in Phoenix, Arizona, with their two sons, Steven and David.

Don't Make Me Smile is the first of three novels by Ms. Park scheduled for publication by Alfred A. Knopf.